LUST IN LATEX

LUST IN LATEX

RUBBER SEX STORIES

EDITED BY
RACHEL KRAMER BUSSEL

Published in the United States by Cleis Press, Inc., 2246 Sixth Street, Berkeley, California 94710.

Printed in the United States.
Cover design: Scott Idleman/Blink
Cover photograph: Roman Kasperski
Text design: Frank Wiedemann

First Edition.
10 9 8 7 6 5 4 3 2 1

Trade paper ISBN: 978-1-62778-004-9
E-book ISBN: 978-1-62778-017-9

Contents

INTRODUCTION: SLEEK, SHINY, SINFUL AND SEDUCTIVE

The first time I tried on a latex dress, I couldn't stop feeling myself up. After being generously shined to a high gloss, the gorgeous red dress gleamed—and so did I. It clung to my body in a way that let me see my curves anew, and any extra flesh I'd lamented carrying suddenly became more fodder for this voluptuous material to caress. It made me proud of my full breasts, wide hips and plump ass because I knew each beckoned to anyone looking. It was way better than being naked, and it felt divine, like I was trapped inside this sleek, erotic cave, and I never wanted to get out. For the characters you'll read about in *Lust in Latex*, rubber, latex and PVC set them off in a similar way, igniting multiple senses and firing up powerful fetishes. They interact with these materials as if they were lovers themselves, and when they meet someone who shares their interest, watch out.

I had expected to get stories about dressing up—sexy nights on the town, glamorous parties, sensuous shopping sprees. And

I certainly did; here you'll read about trying on the outfit of your dreams and realizing its full sexual potential. "In that shiny black PVC dress, she became Carrie the seductress. Carrie the bad girl. Carrie the slut," writes Kristina Wright in the opening story, capturing the way a single slinky outfit can transform a woman into her rightful kinky persona. That these outfits have a life of their own, and are players in these stories just as much, if not more than, their human counterparts, should not surprise you.

It shouldn't have surprised me, but I was caught off guard by the large number of stories I was sent that featured rubber or latex panties. Yet it makes perfect sense: where else would a girl thrill to feel that ultratight, sleek sensation than against her most tender parts? As Elizabeth Coldwell writes in "Cinema Show," "I wriggled in my rubber panties, feeling them rub against my sensitized skin, stimulating me beyond endurance. I stifled a whimper; there was no one sitting next to us, but I didn't want to alert anyone in the rows in front or behind to what was happening."

Another appeal of latex is its translucence; body parts press against it—hard nipples, the outline of a cock or a pussy—and what you can't fully see, you can more than imagine. In "Lick of Pain," Crystal Barela's perfectly kinky lesbian latex tale, she describes it thusly:

> *A cocoon of shiny red brilliance covered Sylvia from ankle to chin. The latex was thin enough for me to see the belt and buckles of her strap-on. Two perfectly round holes were cut into the bodice of the dress and there her turgid nipples were made burgundy where they pressed through the openings. She looked sticky, like a giant wet lollipop. I swallowed hard, hoping my*

> *mouth was worthy of the task, that I could wrap my*
> *tongue around her body and slurp Sylvia between my*
> *plump lips, suck her from head to toe all at once. The*
> *taste of rubber would coat my insides like a balm.*

Other authors tackle the unusual ways rubber and latex can transport us out of the everyday and into a purely fetishized universe. Thomas S. Roche depicts a very hot scene with a vac bed (see vacbed.com for some visuals to accompany your reading), a latex bed in which one can be entirely encased, with strategic openings for maximum arousal. Jeremy Edwards' protagonist in "Tire Stud" gets off on the smell, feel, and look of those round treads, and proves that they don't belong only on vehicles.

The way rubber, latex, and PVC cling to the body—so tight there's no give, room only perhaps for some powder or the trickle of wetness to sneak in between—creates a second skin like no other. A lover is almost battling against the material to get to the prize beneath it, and the look of a nipple or an ass, a cock or a cunt bared beneath such suctionlike material, is enough to make these characters want their lovers to wear it all the time.

Whether you've experienced this intimate, intense molding of skin to rubber yourself, or have simply admired those who choose to adorn themselves in these magical, sex-laden outfits, you're in for a treat.

Rachel Kramer Bussel
New York City

THE DRESS

Kristina Wright

The dress made her do it.

It hung in the back of Carrie's closet, hidden behind silk blouses, pinstriped pants, tailored suits, summer skirts and polo shirts. It languished there in the farthest corner of the closet while other clothes were worn for business meetings and tennis matches and birthday parties and lunches with friends. The dress stayed there when other clothes were tossed in the donation bag, when other new outfits replaced old, when seasons changed and wool trousers were chosen over capri pants. The dress was like an old friend, waiting patiently for a long overdue call.

Finally, after months, the call came.

When Carrie put the dress on, she felt like a different person. She *was* a different person. She wasn't Carrie the junior attorney at the law firm or Carrie the fitness freak or Carrie the buddy who was like one of the guys. In that shiny black PVC dress, she became Carrie the seductress. Carrie the bad girl. Carrie the slut.

She prepared for her night out like a bride preparing for her wedding day. She was shaved, moisturized, perfumed, adorned. She put the dress on, surprised for a moment at how formfitting it was. She wore it only occasionally, once every three or four months, and she was always surprised by how it hugged her body. Her other clothes fit comfortably, making her hardly aware she was wearing them. She never forgot she was wearing the dress. It made her stand up straighter, suck in her stomach, thrust out her breasts that were barely contained by the corset-style bodice—and that was just while she was standing in the privacy of her own bedroom admiring herself in the mirror. Out in public, the dress made her *strut*.

By the time she got to the club, her whole body was throbbing with an intense energy, already anticipating things to come. It wasn't a club she went to often. It wasn't in the best part of town and it appealed to a crowd that was a little more...out there than the sort of people she usually hung with. She wasn't in the mood for the khakis and cappuccino crowd tonight. She wasn't interested in talking politics, 401(k) plans or who was getting married or who was expecting yet another baby. Tonight she wanted to be someone else: the slut in the dress.

She was rewarded for her efforts the minute she walked into the noisy, crowded club. Not everyone stopped to look at the redhead in the black, skintight vinyl dress that laced down to her belly button, but enough people did look—men and women—to give her a little rush. It was the dress, she knew. It didn't hurt that she had the body to fill it out, of course, but the dress commanded attention in a way Carrie alone never could. The four-inch patent leather heels didn't hurt, either. They made her already long legs look like they went on for miles, and not a man in the room could look at the shoes that matched the dress and not wonder what they would look like on the floor next to his bed.

Fending off a couple of overeager guys, Carrie made her way to the bar. The bar spanned the length of one side of the club and it was standing room only. Miraculously, as soon as she approached, a space opened up for her. She thanked the two guys on either side of her and ordered a martini.

"That's on me," said the guy to the left of her.

"Thanks." Carrie gave him a predatory smile, feeling infused with power. "But I'm not going to fuck you."

The guy on her right laughed. "Guess she told you."

Carrie took a long sip of the martini that appeared in front of her in record time, letting her tongue linger on the rim of the glass. Then she smiled. "I'm not going to fuck you, either."

It probably wasn't the wisest thing to say to two guys in a seedy nightclub who both seemed a little inebriated, but the dress made her say and do things that weren't very wise. Like a suit of armor or a protective shield, the dress gave her power and authority. Instead of turning nasty, both men smiled good-naturedly and shrugged.

By the time she finished her second martini, courtesy of the guy on the right simply because he wanted to appear to be a gentleman, Carrie was ready to mingle. She excused herself to her self-appointed guardians with a wink and a "Thanks for the drinks, boys," and disappeared onto the crowded dance floor before either could follow and press the issue.

The music was heavy, throbbing techno with some retro punk thrown in for good measure. It wasn't dancing music, it was *grinding* music, and the crowd writhed on the packed dance floor in pairs and threesomes in alcohol-and-lust-fueled orgiastic bliss. Carrie didn't dance alone for long. Soon she felt the press of a body behind her. A male body. She turned in the circle of his arms and gave him a feral smile.

Her smile faded when she realized she was looking up into

the face of Reynolds, one of the partners at the firm. She wracked her brain for his first name and came up blank. She didn't know him personally; the firm she worked for was one of the largest in the state, with two dozen partners and a hundred or more support staff, but they'd crossed paths a couple of times and he was attractive enough for her to notice him. Dark eyes, dark hair, older than her, but with a boyish appeal that made it hard to peg his age. Of course, she'd never seen him in a social setting wearing low-slung jeans and a T-shirt that clung to his sculpted torso.

She realized his expression hadn't changed—he was still looking at her like he wanted to devour her—and it dawned on her that he had no reason to recognize her, especially in the dress. She was as professional and proper at work as any attorney and, out of that familiar setting and in a dress meant for a vamp, she probably didn't look like the Carrie he might remember on a good day.

"Love the dress," he said, his hand gliding over the slippery PVC from her waist to her hip. "You're stunning."

She smiled again, regaining her composure. The patent leather heels made her almost his height, so she leaned forward until her lips were nearly touching his ear. "Thanks."

"Want to dance?"

She put her arm around his neck and pressed her body against him, rubbing her crotch against his hip in a smooth, sinuous rhythm. "Sure."

He pulled her close and rubbed his erection against her. "Want to go home with me?"

She shook her head. "I don't think so."

He laughed. "Well then, will you at least dance with me until my dick deflates a little?"

She pressed against him, her breasts threatening to burst out of the top of the dress. "What are the odds of that while I'm here?"

"Good point."

She smiled. "C'mon," she said, taking him by the hand.

"Where?"

She just arched an eyebrow at him.

"Yes, ma'am."

She led him outside into the cool night air that made her nipples pucker and raised goose bumps on her bare arms and legs. The parking lot was quiet except for a couple of giggling women hanging drunkenly on each other. Carrie's heart hammered in her chest as she led Reynolds around the side of the club, dark but for the red light cast by an emergency exit sign. She took a deep breath. Knowing there was a chance they could get caught was part of the thrill.

"What are you up to?"

She responded by pressing him up against the wall of the club and kissing him. Hard. She reached down and stroked his cock through his jeans, pleased that it was stiff and thick. He moaned into her when she squeezed him.

Reynolds pulled away. "Are you sure you don't want to go to my place?"

She unzipped his jeans. "I can't wait."

She knelt in front of him, the dress riding up so that she could feel the night air on her ass. She unfastened his jeans and pulled his cock free. It was beautiful and thick. She whimpered in anticipation.

"Please, baby."

She didn't move, not even when he wrapped her long hair in his fist and tried to guide her to his cock. She resisted, knowing he was hers.

"Please," he pleaded again.

She indulged him not because he begged, but because she couldn't stand not having him in her mouth a minute longer. Precome glistened on the tip of his cock like a freshwater pearl and she swirled her tongue around the engorged head, pulling it into her mouth.

He gasped at the contact and thrust his hips forward.

With excruciating slowness that teased them both, she licked his cock from tip to base, fondling his heavy balls with one hand while guiding his cock between her lips with the other. She sucked the head into her mouth and cradled it in the hollow of her tongue, holding it there until he impatiently moved his hips. His hands were slack in her hair, as if he'd forgotten—or didn't realize—he could have some measure of control. Carrie didn't want him to have control. She wanted the power to give him pleasure, but only when she was ready.

Despite their risky location, she took her time sucking him. She lowered her mouth over his cock, relaxing her throat until she had taken as much of him as she could handle without gagging. Then she slid back slowly, revealing his slick, shiny cock. Over and over she deep-throated him until they were both panting, and she knew he was close to orgasm by the way his cock practically leaked precome in a steady stream.

He protested softly when she released his cock long enough to untie the laces that held the bodice of her dress together. "I want you to fuck my tits," she said.

He switched his focus from her mouth to her breasts as she pulled them free from the dress. Her skin was ethereally pale against the black PVC, her nipples hard and dark. She cupped her breasts in her hands, presenting them to him like a gift.

He didn't speak. He took his cock in his hand and laid it in the valley she created by pressing her breasts together. His cock was warm and wet from her mouth. She closed her eyes, enjoying the feel of him against her bare skin.

His hands covered hers and he rolled her nipples between his fingers. She moaned, squeezing her breasts around his cock.

"You feel so good," he gasped.

She braced her hands on his thighs as he cupped her breasts around his cock. Looking up into his eyes, she said, "Fuck me."

His expression was primal. Squeezing her breasts around his cock, he fucked her the way she wanted. She rocked back on her heels as he thrust against her harder and harder, fucking her tits as if he were inside her pussy. Her saliva had dried on his cock and the only thing lubricating her breasts was his precome, but it was enough. From his sharp intake of breath, she knew he was going to come.

"Come on my tits."

He moaned, his cock spurting thick, milky semen—once, twice, three times—across her pale breasts and down the front of her vinyl dress. She kept her breasts pressed together, watching as warm rivulets of come gathered there. Finally, when he seemed to be finished, she leaned forward and kissed the tip of his cock, tasting him.

He released his iron grip on her hair and helped her up. "That was incredible," he said as he tucked his cock back in his pants and straightened his clothes.

Carrie did the same with her sticky breasts, not bothering to lace the bodice of her dress. "Yes, it was."

"I feel bad I didn't do anything for you."

She smiled. She'd wanted to rub her very wet pussy while he fucked her, but she'd been so mesmerized by watching him, she hadn't been able to do anything else. Her pussy still felt engorged but, somehow, watching him come had taken the edge off a little bit. "You'd be surprised what that did for me."

"Oh really?" He started to pull her close, then stopped short. "Oh, man, I am *all* over your dress."

She looked down and saw that he was right. His come glistened in streaks on the already shiny vinyl, leaving no doubt as to what she'd been doing. She laughed. "It's all right, it wipes right off."

"Sounds like the voice of experience." Rather than disapproving, he sounded aroused by the idea. "You're a very bad girl."

There was no reason to tell him she wasn't as bad a bad girl as he thought her to be. No reason to ruin his fantasy—or her own. "I don't suck and tell," she said with a wink.

A burst of laughter startled them both and Carrie decided she'd pushed her luck far enough for one night. She let Reynolds escort her to her car.

"Thanks, really."

"Thank *you*," she said, and meant it sincerely. There was no doubt in her mind that she'd spend many long morning commutes thinking about her escapade with Reynolds. But first, she'd spend a long, leisurely bath masturbating until her pussy was raw while she thought about his thick cock coming between her breasts.

"So, do you think I can see you again or was this a one-time thing?"

"What's your name?"

"Derrick Reynolds," he said.

Right. Derrick. She didn't know why she hadn't remembered. "Well, Derrick, I have no doubt I'll see you again, but I don't know if this is a one-time thing or not."

She left him then, with a furrow between his brow and a limp cock between his legs. The dress had made her do it, and she had no doubt she'd do it again. Maybe even with Derrick Reynolds.

IN A SINGLE BOUND

Shanna Germain

I bet I look stupid," Becca said.

"You look like a superhero." Jon wrapped a strip of latex beneath her breasts and stuck it together in the back. The contrast of the black latex against her pale skin, and the way the strips pushed her breasts up, made them look round and full. Still, she wasn't sure about all the strips of latex that circled her body.

"No superhero in the history of the world ran around wearing this," she said.

"Really?" Jon peeled another strip of latex off the roll and tore it with his teeth. Becca caught a glimpse of something flashing in his blue eyes—was he laughing at her? "You didn't read that comic when you were in high school? The one where all the hot superchicks get their suits cut off and then they get bound up with the leftover strips?"

He *was* laughing at her. The jerk.

"No," she said. "I think you made that one up in your wild youth."

"Yeah, me and every other seventeen-year-old on the planet," he said. "God, I used to dream about this…but I never could decide. Be the villain, just so I could truss a woman up like this? Or be the superhero, so I could set her free?"

The way his blue eyes looked at her, filled with love and a fair bit of greed—that right there was why she'd agreed to this tape thing. She loved latex almost as much as Jon did; the way it captured her skin, the odd combination of softness and strength. And she knew she had the body for it—curvy, but muscular; high, small boobs; long legs. Over the years, Jon had bought her a variety of outfits: latex dresses and corsets that did more than skim her dips and swells, they heightened them, made them superreal. And latex panties. All she had to do was step into a pair—crotchless, backless, a tiny black thong—and she'd be wet in a second. She loved to wear them under regular clothes. Her secret. Hers and Jon's.

But latex tape? When Jon had brought the roll home, she'd laughed. It looked like electrical tape. Or some kind of torturous hair-removal device. But Jon had wrapped her wrist with it, shown her how it just stuck to itself. "People make duct tape outfits all the time," he'd said. And she had to admit the shiny black *was* such a great contrast with her pale skin. Still, being trussed up like some seventeen-year-old's version of a superhero wasn't exactly her fantasy. Worse yet, she was afraid she looked less like a woman of steel and more like a zebra.

Not to mention that Jon wasn't exactly known for his dress-making skills.

"Nervous?" he asked.

He always could tell what she was thinking. "I didn't know one of your superpowers was mind reading," she said.

"I'm not the superhero. You are," he said. "Just a lucky

guess. However…" He used his fingernail to find the end of the tape on the roll. "I do have one special power."

"What's that?"

"You'll have to wait and see."

Jon looped the piece of latex just above her breasts, making them pop out even more. Her nipples, which seemed, somehow, to become a little harder every time he added another bit of tape, now pointed almost skyward.

"Up, up, and away," he said with a grin. She would have hated him, but he licked his thumb and ran it over her nipple as he said it. She tried not to moan. "See, what'd I tell you?" he said. "Superhero."

"Yeah, well, I feel like a super dork."

"You shouldn't," Jon said. "Turn."

She tried to twirl in front of him, although it was more like an egg-wobble. At least she didn't fall down. Between the black latex strips he'd wrapped around her body, the shiny black heels, and that fact that her hands were tied behind her back, her movements weren't exactly graceful.

"Well, I could put a big black *SD* on your chest," Jon suggested as he knelt behind her and looped a latex strip around one thigh. "Suuuper Dork!"

"I could kill you now," she said, but she couldn't help laughing. She would have slugged him, but the latex bow he'd used on her wrists was too strong to break.

"It was just a suggestion," he said. "Turn again."

"Just a bad one." She turned, a little more smoothly this time, until she was facing him.

"You're going to have to spread your legs a little, hon," Jon said. He was so close to her that she could feel his breath between her thighs.

Becca closed her eyes as Jon's fingers worked to wrap the

tape around the uppermost part of her thighs. The sound of the tape rolling off the roll, the *riiip* as Jon used his teeth to tear off strips, all excited her more than she would have expected. Even the feel of his fingers between her thighs, the slick smoothness of the latex against her skin, was turning her on.

"I'm glad you shaved," he said.

Becca barely had time to register that before Jon slid a bit of latex across her clit. She'd never felt anything so soft, so silky, against her. The feel of it made her head swim, and she wished for something to lean back on.

"In or around?" he asked.

"Huh?" She tried to focus as his warm fingers and the cool latex alternated against her.

"Do you want the latex to run on either side, or do you want it to go across the middle?"

It was the first option he'd given her since he'd started dressing her. Or trussing her, rather.

"Uh, around, please," she said, and then felt his fingers work the tape on either side of her shaved lips. He pulled upward on the tape, which pulled her lips apart, and opened the inside of her to the air.

"Like this?" he asked.

She could only nod. Her clit felt slick and wet; she was sure Jon had noticed. While he worked, his fingers skimmed her lips and clit, so lightly they could have been touching her by accident. Jon moved upward, attaching the strips to the one that already circled low around her waist, creating something that was vaguely like underwear—crotchless, backless, sideless, latex strip underwear. If this was what superheroes wore under their costumes, it would certainly explain their lack of panty lines.

Becca shivered as Jon tucked the final strip into her waist.

"All this work, Jon?" Becca said. She found that her tongue

wanted to do things other than talk. It was tripping over itself in her mouth. "All this work just to peel it off in three seconds?"

"Three seconds? Is that what you think of my sexual prowess? I would think you'd know me better by now."

"The ninety-dollar corset?" she asked. God, that had been a beautiful piece of work, but he'd popped all the intricate buttons right off before she'd even gotten inside the house.

"I was overcome by desire," he said.

He adjusted a piece of the latex that formed her underwear, brushing his thumb across her clit as he did so. Becca inhaled sharply.

"What about those great thigh-highs?"

"The boots? I didn't—"

"No, the stocking-things."

Jon slid his fingers from her clit back toward her ass. "I *had* to cut those off. C'mon, they were made for that. Christ, they should have included a pair of scissors in the package."

"You used a knife," Becca said.

Jon's thumb, wet from its ride across Becca's center, found her asshole and pressed. "What?" he asked.

"Oh, oh...forget it," Becca said.

"That's what I thought." Jon stood up and took a step back from Becca. "Jesus, you look amazing."

She missed his hands on her. "Amazing like 'Suuuper Dork!'?" she mimicked Jon's voice. "Or amazing like *amazing?*"

"Yes," Jon said. He pressed his hips against her so she could feel what he thought of it. His hard cock pressed through his jeans into her leg. "Amazing," he whispered. The sound of his voice and the hard length of him gave her a sense of vertigo, as though she wasn't touching the ground.

Then he went on his knees in front of her. His tongue flicked her wet clit while his fingers stroked her, front to back. She forgot about the latex, she forgot she was standing in heels, she forgot everything except his tongue against her. If her hands had been free, she would have taken his head, forced him to bring her to orgasm. As it was, all she could do was push against his mouth, his tongue, begging him with her body.

"Is…is that your superpower?" she asked him.

"Ka-pow," he whispered against her. She could feel his smile. It made her want him all the more, made her ache for him to use his fingers and tongue to finish her.

He stood up, leaving her clit punching with desire.

"Wait, I'm not…I didn't…" Becca pouted. "Your superpower sucks." He just grinned at her—he'd known she hadn't come.

"That's only the beginning," he said. "First, I want you to see how amazing you look." He grabbed the full-length mirror and flipped it around. "Woman of steel," he said.

Becca was in the mirror. Her, only not her. The black latex made her pale skin glisten and glow. It arched her breasts higher and narrowed in her curves. She looked powerful. Stacked. Jon was right: she did look like a superhero. But she also looked like a criminal—bad-ass, even with her hands behind her back.

"Wow," she said. "Where's my cape, though?"

Jon stripped and then stepped behind her. He held on to her wrists with one hand and his erection pressed into the crack of her ass. "I'm your cape, hon," he said. "And if you give me a minute, I bet I can even make you fly."

RUBBER NECKING

Alison Tyler

The sex toy store was on my daily route to work—the curve of the wall of windows traveling with me, the way the silvery face of the full moon used to seem to follow me when I was a kid. I'd sit in my car, stopped in early morning Los Angeles traffic, and I'd do my best not to rubberneck.

Yet, the windows beckoned—the displays dazzling behind the shiny sheets of glass. Corsets made of cobalt satin over fine black boning. Stockings in more than a rainbow of hues—gold, fuchsia, and celadon in fishnet, patterns, and lace. Toys hanging from nets and clotheslines strung from wall to wall, like an X-rated fisherman's haul or an indecent day at the laundromat. And then there was the rubber. A whole window devoted to items made from this stretchy material, matte or shiny, glistening beneath the halogen lamps.

On lucky days, I caught sight of the tall, dark-haired man who changed the displays, watched as he rearranged items or created whole new features—themes for the holidays, or entire windows devoted to a single color. He wore all black, all the time, like so many of the boys in West Hollywood, and he had long, glossy hair, either pulled back in a ponytail, or left down so that it partly curtained his face. He never turned to look at the traffic, paying attention to his job, creating visions out of the risqué materials; stepping back to observe, then continuing, almost as if there was no world outside of the windows.

I enjoyed the lingerie, the pretty frilly items. I liked to look at the sex toys, the cuffs and blindfolds, gags, paddles, and masks. But the rubber items, *those* were the ones that stretched over my day, snapping through my mind when I least expected it. Anything, everything, could take me back to those windows.

The lemon yellow dishwashing gloves resting innocently on the stainless-steel sink in the break room would make me think of elbow-length black rubber gloves I'd seen pinned to a wall in that window. A ball of multicolored rubber bands residing lazily on a coworker's desk would remind me of a red rubber ball gag strapped to the face of an unseeing mannequin. The burnt-licorice scent of tires as I walked through the parking garage would make me want to press my nose to the window shielding the displays and see if I could inhale the scent through that wall of glass. The visions built within me, until I could hardly wait each day to get back home to my empty apartment, to my world of privacy.

Keys thrown onto the coffee table. Pencil skirt discarded on the way down the hall. A shoe here. A shoe there. A rabid rush to the center of the mattress, to the safety of my own fantasy world.

Once on the bed, I could slow down once more, reach for the box hidden in my nightstand drawer. A shake of cornstarch from a bottle by my lamp would help those thin white rubber gloves slide on smoothly, but I would take my time anyway. Making sure to smooth out any wrinkles, growing wetter with the caress of the rubber around each fingertip. When the gloves were fully on, I would interlace my fingers, watching rubber meet rubber.

Now, it would become more difficult to go slowly. With hands that were like someone else's, some stranger's, I would touch myself while I recreated the window displays in my mind. Fingers gliding over my breasts, I imagined the window dresser—with his long dark hair and slim body—dressing *me* in the pale orange rubber sheath he'd slid on a mannequin the week before. Or slipping me into sleek scarlet rubber boots that would reach past my knees. I could see him buckling that bright red ball gag into place between my own parted lips, knew somehow what that sensation would be like, what I would look like, gagged like that.

I spread out my favorite visions, extending them to the breaking point. Me in those boots and a matching coat made of vinyl, a coat with a sheen so bright, the vinyl surface would appear just begging to be come on. I could see the man dressing me in the full-body sleep sack made entirely of heavy-duty rubber, then pressing himself against me when I couldn't move at all, his naked body against mine clad all in rubber. The shudders would start to work through me.

What would his hands smell like after working with rubber all day?

Would I be able to lick his fingers and taste the bitterness on them?

Oh, yes, I could imagine that as well, me on my knees in front of him, sucking his finger into my mouth, swirling my tongue around it. My own fingers, encased in that thinnest sheen of rubber, would probe and tickle my clit—rubber on wetness now—until the climax came and took me away.

And then, disgusted with myself, I'd tear off the stretchy

gloves and ball them up, throwing them in a corner in a fit of temper. I'd dispose of them the next day between thumb and pointer, as if to say, "That's that. I never have to do *that* again." But I'd know the whole time that I would be driving past the store once more; know, more honestly, that a whole box of rubber gloves lay waiting in my drawer: one hundred gloves in a box, with a spare box behind, unopened, just in case.

One day, late for work, I found myself cruising toward the store with ease. No bottleneck today, which meant no rubbernecking for me, sitting in a traffic jam, watching the windows. As I drove by, I caught a quick blur of him, the dark-haired man changing the displays, peeling the orange rubber dress off the model, painstakingly revealing her plastic body as the dress begrudgingly gave way.

I craned my head to see, and that's precisely when the traffic stopped, and I slammed into the car in front of me.

L.A. drivers collect accidents like some people notch lovers on their headboards. This was a minor scrape and tussle, not even damaging enough to properly be called a fender bender, but that didn't stop the rubberneckers from watching. Didn't stop the window dresser from pausing in his motion to check out the action, so that for once I saw his full face clearly: the strong lines of his cheekbones, the glint of a silver ring in his lower lip, the dark brows, the furrow in his forehead.

I pulled my car to the side of Santa Monica Boulevard and exchanged phone numbers and insurance information with the annoyed soccer mom whose dragon-red Hummer I'd scratched. Then I sat in my car and stared at the steering wheel. Something had to give. I'd have to change my route, throw away that secret stash of rubber gloves...

Suddenly, there was a rap on the passenger window. I

looked up, dazed, to see the window dresser motioning for me to roll down my window. For a moment, I couldn't remember how to turn on the ignition. But I got the job done, pressed the control button on my armrest, and watched the window slide down.

"You okay?"

I nodded.

"No offense," he said, his deep voice sounding concerned, dark eyes watching. "But you don't really look okay."

I was staring behind him, at the display window, the mannequin still only half-dressed, her orange rubber sheath pulled down to reveal molded, nipple-less breasts. I wanted to be wearing that dress, wanted this dark-eyed man to be peeling it off me.

No, that wasn't right.

I wanted him to be putting it on me. In that window. While other drivers slid past.

"Come on out," he said, gesturing. "Let me get you a glass of water. Cup of coffee. Something."

Something was the word that lingered. *Something* was what I wanted.

I followed him into the store, around the racks and shelves and stacks, to the back room, so much like the break room at my own office, down to the pair of yellow rubber gloves resting on a stainless steel sink. I watched him pour me a cup of coffee from the pot on the counter, and then smile at me as I drank my first trembling sip.

"You're a virgin?"

I stared at him, wild-eyed. What was he saying? I'd fallen down a rabbit hole and ended up where?

"First traffic accident?"

Now, I had to smile. "How'd you know?"

"You just seem more shaken up than most people. I catch a lot of accidents out the window. Generally, drivers just go on their way. Some never even hang up the phone during the whole interchange."

"I'm a pretty careful person," I said, and realized that summed up my life in so many different ways. Careful. Careful never to let on what I want, what I'm like, what I do when I'm all by myself.

He laughed, "I'm care*less*," he said. "We'd probably make a good team. Balance each other out."

Yes, I thought. *You'd put the dress on me, and I'd stay still for you. You'd peel it off again, the rubber sticking to my skin, and I'd...*

He was looking at me oddly. Had I said the fantasy out loud? No, he was looking at my wrists, the two rubber bands I wore there, my one public weakness. Anyone could have grabbed a rubber band, right? Nothing strange about—

He came forward, slid his fingertips under the red rubber band on top, snapped once, and I shuddered. "Windows go two ways," he said. "You know?"

My eyes couldn't have gotten larger. I just stared at him.

"I've seen you watching, in your little blue Prius. You stare at me when I'm changing the displays. The rubber ones, right?"

Oh, God. I needed to get out, to leave quickly. My heart was pounding. *Thanks for the coffee* was on my lips, but he stopped me.

"Don't worry, Casey."

"How'd you know my name?" I was stammering.

"I came out of the store as soon as you had the accident, and I heard you when you were exchanging information."

I'd been so consumed by what I'd done that I hadn't even noticed him. My eyes roamed the room. I felt panicky and I put my hand out, intending to rest my palm on the back of the nearest chair, but as I did so, he reached for my hand instead. Reached and held. He smiled, and I realized now that his dark eyes weren't brown, but the deepest purple-tinted blue. "Jarred," he said, touching his chest, and then adding, "I've got something to show you."

Etchings, I thought wildly. *He's going to show me his etchings, isn't that what men are always showing women?* And then I laughed, because this was all so surreal. On the one day when I managed to avoid traffic, I had wound up in an accident. On the one day when I had finally assured myself that I was over this need, this craving, I had wound up in the center of my own fetish-filled universe. Because where Jarred was leading me was the window. The window with the mannequin, still half-dressed, her hard body smooth and pale beneath the hot lights, showing no signs of modesty at all.

"*This* is what you like, right?"

He peeled the dress the rest of the way off her, working it free from her body. I heard that sticky, sucking sound of rubber being pulled from plastic, and I thought I might come right then.

"Most people can't wear orange, but I know you can."

What did he want me to do? What was he suggesting?

He held the dress out to me, and I shook my head, legs quavering.

"People will see."

"Yes," he said, as if he didn't understand why that would be a problem. No, as if it weren't a problem at all.

I took the dress with trembling hands. The rubber was warm from being under the lights. The orange was more peach than traffic-cone neon. He was right. The color would work for me, with my gold-brown hair, light-brown eyes, tanned skin. But how would I put it on? Where?

Jarred seemed to be waiting for me, and then he snapped his fingers. "Wait."

He hurried from the window, and I was left to stand there, totally still, like the naked mannequin at my side. I saw the traffic coasting by from Jarred's point of view, and I realized that I had been as on display to him as he had been to me. There were mirrors in the window. He would have seen my reflection, or turned to look when I hadn't noticed, when I'd been captivated by the clothes and accessories rather than the man in charge.

That man stepped back into the window now, with a shaker in his hand. "Cornstarch," he said, and I nodded, knowing what to do. What he wanted. And yet...

"I'll block you," he said, stepping in front of my body, facing away. I took a deep breath. I thought about the box of rubber gloves next to my bed, thought about the routine I went through every single night. Then, quickly, I peeled off my jacket and unzipped my navy blue dress. I wasn't wearing stockings, just a bra and panties in a neutral beige, easy to remove. I shook a bit of the cornstarch on my palms and spread it over my body, growing more confident somehow with that little shake of fairy dust, and then I lifted the dress and slowly began to slide it up.

The rubber gave, moving over my curves, fitting itself instantly to my body. I pulled it, tugged the arm straps open so I could slide my arms through one at a time—a full-size Barbie in rubber fetish gear.

Jarred seemed to know the precise moment to turn back around. Just as I stepped back into my black pumps, he faced me, and I saw the light in his eyes as he admired the rubber dress now shielding my naked skin.

He came forward then, putting his arms around me, kissing me softly on the lips, then on the neck, then bending on his knees to kiss me through the rubber of the dress. I put my hands on his shoulders to keep myself steady. My eyes were wide open, and I stared out the window as his lips met my pussy sheathed in that supple rubber. I saw a blur out the window, heard the squeal of tires as a passing car slammed to a stop, heard the crumple of metal as the car behind failed to put on the brakes in time.

"Rubberneckers," Jarred said softly.

I nodded, as my mind stretched the word taut and found the term fit just right.

SLICKER THAN SLIK

Radclyffe

promise it won't hurt, baby," Tina said as she leaned in the doorway of the bathroom, her hips cocked and a razor dangling seductively between her fingers. It helped that she didn't have any clothes on, but not all that much. If I could have kept my attention on her tits, round and firm and just right for squeezing, or her sleek belly and high tight ass, I would have been fine. But the little steel blades of the razor glinted and I couldn't take my eyes off it.

"I'll suck you off when we're done," she coaxed.

"You better do more than that," I muttered. I did not shave my cunt. That was a girl thing. Trim, maybe, sure. Tina liked it when I trimmed. She said it was easier to find my clit, and believe me, anything that got her hot mouth cinched around my stiff clit worked for me. She gives the best head of any femme I've ever met.

"And after that, I've got a surprise for you." Tina showed me a tiny bit of tongue.

"If it involves you strapping it on and fucking me, forget it."
But I was grinning, too. She'd been wanting to flip me forever,
and to tell you the truth, the idea had its appeal. Whenever I let
her top me she got this intense look on her face, like every move
was the most important thing she'd ever done. When she pushed
her fingers inside me, her eyes got big, like she'd just discovered the secret to the universe. And when she made me come,
as much of her hand crammed into me as she could get and her
thumb beating my hard-on and me yelling my head off, she'd
laugh out loud as if she'd just been given the best present of her
life. So let's just say I could be persuaded. Pretty easily. But she
didn't need to know that.

"What sort of surprise?" I was still playing unconvinced.

"As soon as we finish, I'll show you," Tina said. "I've got this
incredibly cool outfit for you to wear to the party."

"Explain why that requires shaving." I crossed my arms and
pretended to resist. The fact is, anything she wants from me, she
gets. And not just because of the sex, but that's another story.

"You'll see. Come on, Dannie, you promised I could dress
you up for my birthday."

Yeah, sure I promised, when she had her little finger tickling the inside of my asshole and her tongue making fast figure
eights around the head of my clit. I'd needed to come so bad I'd
have agreed to march down Market Street in a frilly apron and
nothing else at that point. I sighed.

"Okay, but be careful. No nicks. And, Jesus, watch my
clit."

She perched me on the edge of the tub and lathered me up
with warm water and shaving cream, and she was careful. The
biggest problem was that she couldn't shave me without touching
me—stretching my lips out to get in the crevices, pressing down
on my shaft to get that little cleft right at the base, and generally

tugging and pushing and pulling all the parts that are hot-wired right to my clit. By the time she was done washing the soap off and patting me dry, my cunt was smooth and my clit stood straight up like a fat, red thumb.

"Suck it, baby," I whispered, looking down as she knelt on the floor between my spread legs, her face just inches from my crotch.

She smiled sweetly, pursed her lips, and sucked my clit all the way in to the root. My legs shot out straight when the tip of her tongue poked underneath the hood. I mumbled a lot of "Lick," "Suck," "Oh, Jesus, that's good," and "Please, baby, do me there," while trying not to come. Watching her suck on my clit like it was a Tootsie Pop usually makes me shoot off right away, and I was already making those girlie sounds I can't help making when I'm about to come. She was stretching it out like plump taffy, her red lips sliding around the purple head, tugging at the crown with her teeth, and I felt the tight coiling in my cunt break loose and whisper down along my thighs. My clit went rock hard like it does just before it hops and pops.

"Ooo, I'm gonna shoot," I whined.

My clit flew out of her mouth a second before I went off. She sat back on her heels and gazed up at me with her big, brown eyes.

"Not yet." She knows me well and made a quick grab for my hands before I could get my fingers on my clit. A couple of good jerks and I would have come in her face.

"Goddamn it, Tina, I need to get off." I was growling, but I kinda liked it when she made me wait. Sometimes my stomach hurt the next morning from being clenched so tight for so long until she finally let me come.

"Let's go in the bedroom first." She kissed the tip of my clit and

I let out a pathetic whimper. "It's time for your outfit. Come on."

Like I could walk. But I got up on shaky legs, my clit a hot coal in the center of my cunt, and trailed after her into the bedroom like an eager puppy. What can I say? I had a wicked hard-on and she was my salvation.

I didn't see any clothes in the bedroom, and what I did see made me almost forget about my clit. The bed was covered with some kind of plastic sheet. Now I'm up for almost anything, especially on Tina's birthday, but she'd never mentioned water sports before.

"Uh, babe? What's going on?"

"Lie down on your belly," Tina directed. "Are you warm enough?"

"Warm?" I laughed. "I'm about to incinerate. Just do me real fast before we get dressed. It won't take long. I'm ready to pop."

She ran her nails down between my tits, over my belly, and dipped one finger into my cunt. When she rubbed my clit, my legs almost gave out. I grabbed her wrist and tried to shove her hand inside me, but she backed away quickly and pointed to the bed.

"Facedown."

Intrigued despite being slightly pissed that she wouldn't let me come, I stretched out on the cool smooth surface. I turned my head and watched her set out a strange assortment of objects—a stainless-steel bowl, some kind of lotion, and a can of something that I didn't recognize.

"What's all that?"

Tina gave me a look like a little kid at Christmas, excited and pleased with herself. "Your clothes for tonight."

Then she proceeded to open the can and pour a viscous black substance into the stainless steel bowl. She set it aside, picked up the lotion, and sat on the bed beside me. "You'll be wearing a jockstrap and a cropped sleeveless T-shirt."

"I don't get it."

She squirted something cool and thick on my back and started to rub it all over me, concentrating on my shoulders and ass. The second she started touching me, my clit was twitching again.

"Latex body paint." She slid her lubed fingers into the crack of my ass, worked them back and forth, did a quick pass over my cunt, and jerked my clit. "Stay hard for me."

"Oh, yeah," I grunted, humping her fingers. "It's a stone."

"The lotion will help the latex come off later," she said like we were having a normal conversation rather than me about to come all over her hand. She let go of my hard-on and I cried. Real tears leaked out of my eyes.

"I wanna come. I wanna come so bad."

"I know you do. Be good."

My ears were buzzing so loud I couldn't tell what she was doing until I felt her smearing something different on my ass with her fingers, drawing patterns of some kind.

"That looks so cool," Tina said. "I'm painting the jock on with the latex. It's so sexy."

"Can I come?" I was pretty much on a one-way track to anything-you-want-just-please-let-me-shoot by then. I didn't care what she was putting on me or if it ever came off. She smoothed two fingers down between my legs, along the far outside edges of my cunt. I wanted her inside, fucking me, and lifted my ass so she could get to me.

"Stay still, Dannie. I want this to dry smooth. It only takes a minute."

"Rub my clit. Make it shoot. Please, Tina, baby."

She smeared more latex over my ass, then leaned down and

ran her tongue around the inside of my ear. "You can play with it while this dries, but you can't come. I want you to shoot that big load in my mouth."

"Fuck," I muttered, raising up enough to get my fingers around my clit. Nothing feels as good as shooting off in Tina's mouth, and I wasn't gonna settle for creaming in my hand when I could have that. I know how to work a hard-on without losing my load, so I just squeezed and tugged every now and then while this second skin tightened around my ass. I must have been twitching a little too much because Tina kept whispering for me to lie still. Just when I didn't think I could take it any longer, she told me to roll over. As soon as I did, she knelt between my legs and latched on to my nipple with her teeth. That just about finished me, and I would have come except she grabbed my hand and yanked it off my clit.

"Fuck!" I yelled this time.

Laughing, Tina worked my tits over for a few minutes, then spread the lube over my breasts and belly and started with the latex again. This time I could watch her and I almost forgot my aching dick. She scooped handfuls of the stuff onto my tits and smoothed it in swirly circles, using one finger to outline the edges, making it look like a T-shirt that just barely covered my nipples. Then she moved down and painted the waistband of the jock just above my pubes. Or where they used to be. I eased up on my elbows so I could see her slicking her way to my crotch. The latex dried smooth and flat, and when she put a second coat on it looked like clothes you could see through, only not quite. She had everything covered but the few inches right around my clit. That was still poking out like a fat red cherry.

"You're not gonna cover that, are you?"

Instead of answering, Tina ran the flat of her tongue slowly between my cunt lips, sucking up my come and dragging the slightly rough surface of her tongue over the head of my clit. Stars burst behind my eyes and my legs started doing a jittery dance on the rubber sheet.

"I'm gonna coat right up to it," Tina whispered in between licks. "So when you're at the party no one will see your hard-on." She sucked me hard and fast and I started to come. "But I'll know…"

My clit was jerking against her lips and I was making crazy crying sounds.

"…it's right there."

She sucked me in deep so I could finish shooting in her mouth, and then my arms gave out and I fell back in a daze. About all I could move was my tongue, which was a good thing, because Tina flipped around on the bed and straddled my face.

"Lick me off, baby," she purred, and while I did, she kept running her fingers over the black shiny stuff covering my tits and crotch, polishing it up.

"Slick, so slick," she crooned as I sucked and licked her sweet, hard clit. Right before she whimpered and gushed all over my face, she sighed, "Oh, baby, you're slicker than Slik."

STRETCHING LOGIC

Jean Roberta

Maureen tried to give Xavier a wise, motherly look. "You're playing devil's advocate. Again." She picked her cup of coffee up off the table and held it against the delicate pink skin of her cleavage, enjoying the warmth. "I can't believe you really think the U.S. should take over Canada. Especially now."

She twirled a lock of her long chestnut hair around her index finger, looking more flirtatious than she intended. It had been years since Xavier had been her student in a first-year writing class, but she still couldn't quite think of him as her equal. Or so she told herself.

This time, the context was different. They had debated politics, history, the arts, religion, culture and sex roles in their favorite coffee shops while the summer sun baked the pavement outdoors, when golden leaves drifted from the trees, when snow pelted the windows, and when the cool wind of early spring promised better things to come. But Maureen had never invited Xavier to her home alone before.

He was stretching a rubber band to the breaking point, aiming at the shadow between her breasts, just visible above the deep V neckline of her forest green sweater. "I never said they should take over. More the other way 'round. Merging two similar countries would be more efficient than pretending they are completely separate, which is a myth even now. You misunderstand me, Lady Maureen. Do you know how sexy you look?"

"Is that why you're planning to shoot me with an elastic?"

"Right between the tits." He studied her from deep brown eyes, using both long, thin hands to stretch and release the wide rubber band that he had fished from her open briefcase, which sat in its usual place on a chair at her dining-room table. *Snap!* "Think of the sting." He licked his lips. "It could give you a rosy glow."

In the years since they had first met in Maureen's class, Xavier had matured into a confident young man who worked out religiously to maintain his muscle tone. He still had an alert face with prominent cheekbones. His black hair still hung boyishly over his forehead and down his neck, but his hairstyle had evolved from a desperate cover-up for teenage acne to a signature look. In numerous subtle ways, he looked infinitely more adult than he had before.

Maureen secretly found him fascinating. Behind the predictable game-playing of a young man testing his luck was a quick mind as capable of surprises as his body. She had always seen his potential, but she had always buried her sexual interest in him under the calm façade of an intellectual fairy godmother.

"I'm older than you," she told him.

"Pffft. What, you're in hibernation because you're over forty? I like cougars."

"I'm not a cougar! They go hunting in bars."

"Well, I'm a cougar-hunter with my trusty weapon." He

smiled into her eyes and snapped the rubber band against the warm skin where she had pressed her coffee cup.

The slight sting flowed instantly into both her nipples, waking them up. She shifted in her seat, aware that her hardened nipples could be seen through her thin beige bra and clingy sweater.

"You're a brat." She reached for his hands, and he grabbed her wrists. She raised her trapped hands, stood up and leaned forward to push him off, but he pulled her to his chest. Before she could back off, he released her wrists and wrapped his arms around her waist, holding her slight weight securely.

"I'm your disciple and loyal servant, milady. Don't I deserve a reward for my years of devotion?"

She didn't struggle out of his grasp, so he leaned forward and kissed her. It was a soft, deep, satisfying kiss, combining just the right amounts of friendship and passion. He slipped a hot tongue into her mouth, and she didn't bite it. He actually trembled with relief. When he reluctantly pulled away from her, both of them were breathing hard.

"Xavier." The large nipples that crowned her modest but perky breasts pressed into his chest, which was covered with a threadbare T-shirt. Her solid points were not merely philosophical, and Xavier reached up to run his fingers gently over them.

"You want me," he told her. "Say it." As though showing his devotion, he reached under her hair to pull her head toward his lips.

Maureen jumped when he snapped his rubber band close to the back of her neck.

"Heh," he chuckled. "My dear, imagine what it would feel like to be hit by a lot of little rubber catapults. A snap here and a snap there." He playfully snapped his weapon on her shoulder and down her back while she squirmed and squealed like a girl.

"You need that treatment yourself! That's my elastic, you know."

"So you admit it! Why do you have so many in your brief-case, woman? Collecting rubber?"

Maureen stretched her arms around his back, looking at him seriously. She suspected that he had given this topic some thought. "Elastic bands are useful," she explained, as though to a slow learner. "They hold things together. Until they break, anyway. Tell me what you use them for."

"Not them. It, dear woman, the wondrous fruit of the rubber tree. As smooth as an oil slick and as stretchy as a nice, welcoming pussy. I bet you wouldn't have stayed childless all these years if your gentleman friends hadn't dressed their little soldiers in latex suits."

"True," she laughed. "And if you came here for that, I hope you're not going to be too disappointed."

Xavier looked stricken to the heart. "Did I come here to hide the sausage? To tear off a piece? Is that what you think? Perish the thought. I came here to enjoy the company of my beautiful, smart and challenging friend Maureen, whom I want to know as deeply as possible. In the carnal sense, down to the core. I want to hear you scream with pleasure." He reached under her sweater to stroke her back and search for the hooks of her bra.

"Okay. You want to see what's under my clothes and I want to see how you've grown up. I'll take something off and you take something off."

Maureen stepped away from him, ran all her fingers through her glossy brown hair, shook it, and let it fall slowly to her shoulders. Then she grasped the bottom edge of her sweater and pulled up, turning it inside out as she raised it over her head.

Her translucent, seamless bra looked weightless, less a source of support for her breasts than a thin covering like a condom.

Her puckered, deep-pink nipples were clearly visible on her girlish mounds beneath the fabric. "Perfect," he told her. "You should air them out more often."

She shimmied slightly like a stripper, unhooked her bra and tossed it on the table with a broad sweep of her arm. Xavier applauded. "All right!" he said. He bent down with a flourish to kiss each of her nipples.

"My turn," he bragged, grinning uncontrollably. He stood before her, bowed slightly and yanked his T-shirt over his head. After forcefully throwing the faded cotton shirt to the floor, he posed for Maureen, discreetly flexing his arm muscles so that his lightly furred chest rippled and bulged. "You're built, my man," she said. She knew this was what he wanted to hear, and it was true.

"See this?" he asked her, unzipping his jeans. He kicked off his shoes, then stood easily on one foot as he pulled a pant leg off his other leg, then repeated the process with the other pant leg. He threw his jeans into a corner and stood naked except for slick black rubber shorts with an opening that gave his cock room to grow. The gleaming texture of his fancy pants looked hypnotic next to his warm beige skin.

"I'm Captain Goodride, baby," he bragged. "Check it out." He turned around slowly, letting her see the smooth planes of his body from all sides. Then he leaned forward from the waist and shook his ass in her face as well as he could. He managed a sensuous side-to-side undulation.

Maureen slapped one of his buttcheeks, releasing a faintly industrial smell of rubber.

"I'll get you back, Queen Bitch," he threatened cheerfully. He grabbed her around the waist and pulled her roughly to his chest. This time, he pressed his hot lips to hers and ravished her mouth with his tongue. She staggered backward, feeling weak in the knees. He tightened his grip with one hand while using the other to find the back zipper of her linen pants.

Maureen held on to his incredibly hard arms, trusting him to support most of her weight while he undressed her.

She expected Xavier to tease and withhold and make her beg. Instead, he reached down the front of her pants to find her moist bush. "I don't need latex for this," he assured her, sliding two fingers up and down her slit, enjoying the treasure hunt. "No mercy," he explained. "I can't be sure you're not an enemy agent, so I have to make sure you're not carrying any recording devices." Maureen laughed and groaned, remembering their argument about whether their own government did as much spying on its citizens as most others.

Once Xavier had found her clit, he rolled, pinched, squeezed and stretched it. He plunged his two fingers as deeply into her wetness as they would go, then alternated the finger-fuck with the tormenting of her clit. "Oh!" she exhaled, despite her intentions. "Xavier! I'll come!" His strategy was so far from her expectations that she seemed likely to erupt from surprise.

"Giving in so easily?" he taunted. "I bet you can hold out longer than you think. Come on, woman, try it." He continued exploring her depths and coaxing her clit to its ultimate size. She squirmed in his grip, and found that this increased the friction in her most sensitive places, bringing her closer to an explosion.

She yelped when her pussy squeezed on its own, clutching his fingers as though she didn't want him to withdraw. Her spasms seemed to go on forever, although, as her logical consciousness reminded her, they could only have lasted a few minutes at most.

"Good to know what you like," he smirked, pulling her crumpled pants down past her knees, taking her stretch-lace panties down with them. Her own clothes felt ridiculous to her by then, although Xavier's rubber shorts looked as natural on him as the underwear of a rogue spaceship captain.

Maureen tried to fold her pants neatly, but Xavier impatiently grabbed her hand and forced her to drop them. Not wanting to seem like a bully, he took them from her and laid them on a chair. "You want more, girl?" he leered, looking her up and down. "If you want to know what I've got, you have to get these off me." He looked down at the stretched rubber that barely covered the hard bulge of his cock.

He had already scoped out the house, and he knew where he wanted to go. He pulled her, naked and still wet, into her own bedroom.

Above the unmade bed hung a large poster of a woman crouched for action, holding a leather-handled whip with rubber strands. Her tousled brown hair, pale skin and slim body looked like Maureen's. Her intense green eyes stared challengingly at the viewer, giving her face a completely different expression from Maureen's usual guarded smile. The woman's shiny black catsuit clung to every part of her, and it flashed in the moody light from a full moon and a sky full of stars. She stood on gleaming black stilettos, sure of her balance.

"Ah," Xavier acknowledged, apparently to himself. "So where's your suit, honey?"

Maureen's blush spread beyond her face to her upper chest. For once she didn't know what to say. They both knew that she could afford a much more extensive fetish wardrobe than he could. And now they both knew that she was afraid to give in to her deepest desires.

The hunger of her skin and the demanding need in her cunt didn't make her helpless in the hands of a man. Not really. Certainly not in the hands of Xavier, who respected a woman's will and self-knowledge. Only a conventional image of the sanitized professional she stubbornly thought she was supposed to be could defeat her and make her look like a fool in his eyes. He was seeing her without her usual defenses, and she felt totally exposed. "Haven't had time to go shopping," she mumbled.

"Take mine," he dared her, beckoning her on. "Come and get me." He bounced on the balls of his feet, then dashed to the other side of her bed, where he stretched, crouched low, swaying from side to side and posing like a boxer. "I've got a big package for you." He snickered. "But you have to unwrap it."

"I'll peel off your fancy panties, spaceman," she bragged. She ran around her bed and lunged at him, hair flying, while he tried to dodge her. They fell on the bed together and rolled over as she tried to hook her fingers firmly under the waistband of his shorts. He pushed her beneath him and tried to immobilize her, but she rolled away and renewed her grip.

Xavier's slick shorts clung to him like a secret fantasy and resisted Maureen's efforts to peel them off. Her manicured fingernails (one of her little self-indulgences) were no help. Each time she lost her grip, the rubber returned to its original shape with an aggravating snap. She realized that she would have to roll it down, even though Xavier wouldn't stop moving.

Maureen tickled him over the ribs, close to the armpits and on his sensitive belly, keeping him off guard. Then she grabbed his shorts with both hands and rolled. "You can't do it," he gloated. With each roll, the rubber grew less flexible.

"Then I'll do this." With a strength she didn't know she had, she rolled the man himself onto his side. Holding him in place with one hand, she leaned over him to reach the metal-backed hairbrush on her bedside table.

"Bad boy!" She swatted him with the brush as a kind of experiment. She loved the sound of the metal meeting the rubber that covered his tight, muscular ass. The thought flashed into her mind that rubber was actually a hardened liquid, and it could conduct sensation almost as well as water.

Whap! Maureen swung the hairbrush with more confidence.

"Oh, ma'am, I'll be good," whined Xavier, barely suppressing a laugh. He seemed as amused as a spoiled teenager who thinks that his parents will always bail him out of jail, no matter what.

Whap! Whap! Whap! Maureen felt as if she could pull strength from the glorious image on her wall, the unstoppable woman who would never let an opponent or a playmate turn her into a joke. Xavier inhaled sharply, and the sound tickled her.

"You don't get to keep your pants on in my bed, boy." She had just made up this rule, but it sounded sensible to her. *Whap! Whap!* He was obviously feeling her strokes.

"Will you take them off, or do I have to blister your behind?" Glancing at his front, she saw that the bulge at his crotch was bigger than before. *Whap! Whap!* She didn't want to lose the momentum.

"Oh! O-kay, Maureen, yeah, please, okay, jeez, you hit hard." His nose was running and his eyes were damp.

Whap! "One to grow on," she told him. She backed off to let him peel his shorts down.

He rolled onto his hands and knees, and used both hands to pry the rubber away from his sore skin. As the slick black shell came down by inches, she could see the satisfying redness she had left on his buttcheeks. Xavier slid off the bed and stood on the other side to finish peeling off his pants.

For a moment he stood, shorts in hand, with a hard red boner pointing straight at Maureen. "Ma'am," he said respectfully, hardly daring to look at her. He handed her the shorts, and she held them to her nose.

The unmistakable smell of male jizz and crotch-funk mixed with the smell of rubber to form a distinct symphony of aromas that sang of want and need, power and submission. Maureen loved it. Like a finicky cat, she turned the shorts over and licked the crotch, which almost felt steamy from Xavier's body. She trailed her tongue along the poreless and seamless expanse of rubber, leaving a wet streak and watching him watching her.

He seemed to be vibrating. *Captain Goodride,* thought Maureen. She certainly hoped so.

"Good boy," she said, looking at his mutely expressive cock. "We need to dress him up for the party. Open the top drawer."

Xavier obediently opened a bedside table drawer and found a packet of condoms in neon colors and ribbed textures. Not daring to choose for himself, he handed her the whole package.

"Hmm," she muttered, making up her mind. "Purple for you." She ripped open a small packet with her teeth and beckoned Xavier back onto the bed. He understood her.

He lay down carefully on his back and looked up at her expectantly. She was tempted to leave him in suspense, but her own need felt too urgent to be denied much longer. She rolled the latex sheath onto his cock, which jerked slightly at her touch.

Maureen eased herself down on his manly shaft until she felt completely filled. She savored the feeling for a moment, and then began to ride him, first in gentle bounces and then harder, finding her rhythm. She milked him with her inner muscles, and he groaned in delight.

"Maureen! I can't wait!" he warned her.

"Sure you can," she sneered. "Hold it as long as you can."

As she had guessed, this order brought him closer to a crisis point. "Uh!" he grunted. "Lady!" He came in a long gush, keeping his eyes closed as though he preferred to be in the dark when all the sap flowed out of him. While Xavier was melting down, Maureen came again. It was like a quiet sneeze, just enough to take the edge off her need. Desire still hummed under her skin like an electric current. She knew she wasn't finished for the day.

For an instant, Maureen wondered whether come could be used to make anything, and then she realized how silly that thought was. Of course. She wondered briefly what her baby by Xavier would look like, assuming she could still conceive. She decided to file that image away to be studied later. It was the scariest fantasy she could remember having.

Almost reluctantly, she slid off him, collected the limp purple bag of his fluid, and deposited it in the wastebasket. She didn't want their mood to be spoiled by the presence of messy waste products. She wanted more smooth, exhilarating rides.

When she came back to bed, she held him in her arms, and he hugged her as though he never wanted to let go.

"Who would have guessed?" she asked rhetorically.

"Lady Maureen, you are one scary mama. I knew I could unlock your potential." He managed to sound humble but smug.

"*You* unlocked *my* potential?"

"Not all of it. We've just started. You need my help to go for what you really want. You know I'm right." She laughed, not trusting herself to say anything.

He wasn't finished. "You're a woman, not a walking text-book. Not everything you do has to make sense."

"But everything happens for a reason," she corrected him.

She looked at him, and he grinned back at her. He knew that he had stretched his luck, and he was glad. She knew that she had stretched her boundaries and enlarged her future in the process. Maureen and Xavier were both developing a mental image of their relationship as something dark and limitless as outer space, fluid and stretchy and slick and shiny, as bouncy as a ball and as snappy as a rubber band.

They both knew that their next date would be a shopping trip.

TIRE STUD

Jeremy Edwards

As a hard-core environmentalist, I've always felt weird about my obsession with big-ass automotive tires. I never wanted to buy into the Great American Motor Vehicle Fetish…to glamorize these machines that are, at best, a mixed blessing.

But I had to spend a lot of time on the road when I was a traveling saleswoman. My hilarious friends used to kid me about my alleged romps in the hay with farmers' sons. Meanwhile, the reality was that I was fucking truck drivers northbound and southbound on I-95. Inhibitions were broken down in many a breakdown lane, and very little rest was obtained at rest areas.

As for the truck stops, I knew them like the back of my clit. Like anyone who travels for a living, I kept track of the best places to pee. But I also kept track of the best places to give or get head, get stroked against a wall, or do a set of pantyless knee-bends onto some fresh driver dick.

Jesus, I loved the way those places smelled. The aroma of hot truck tire permeated the parking lots and even the insides of the buildings. All around me, I could sense rubber that was as hot as I was. The rational part of me knew that what I was inhaling couldn't possibly be good for the environment. But I couldn't control what it did to my senses—nor, to be honest, would I have wanted to. It acted on me like a drug, making my pulse race and my pussy throb, and I reasoned that as long as I didn't unnecessarily contribute to all this intoxicating toxicity, it couldn't hurt for me to enjoy it for all it was worth, as I slid wetly out of the car in search of my next trucker ride.

By the time I turned thirty, I had settled down a lot. I'd taken a job with a local nonprofit, as I'd always wanted to, and I'd traded in my road-weary Honda for a shiny new laminated bus pass. And though I wasn't exactly what you'd call a celibate, I was on a moderate fuck diet of one or two poets/musicians/activists a month, rather than one or two truck drivers a week. I kind of liked getting old.

But the scent of tire rubber always spelled sex to me. One whiff of a delivery truck on a summer day could take my cunt straight back to my favorite interstate parking lot, and I'd have to head for the nearest ladies' room to do something about it.

The house I rented after I gave up the road life came with a small, shady backyard. And one of the first things I'd done after moving in was install a tire swing on the biggest oak. Recycling, you know. I had total privacy back there, and that tire was my favorite place to jill off. Gently swinging and underwear-free, with the evocative perfume of the rubber wafting into my face, I'd let my fingers find my groove slot, and I'd soon be pounding my ass up and down against the thin air that tickled me from below.

So it wasn't just my environmental conscience that made me an early adopter when those sandals, belts, and other accessories manufactured from recycled tire rubber came on the market.

The only problem was that I couldn't wear, carry, or even look at these items without getting instantly horny. I'm a girl who can smell old tire rubber from across the room.

It's remarkable that I didn't smell Mitch from across town, given his usual attire. When he walked into my neighborhood granola-crunchy café, I practically creamed my favorite junkyard-rescued couch. The dude had tire tread all over his slim, hipster body, from his sandals all the way up to his fucking fedora. Did I mention creaming the couch?

He had obviously crafted most of the outfit himself. (Believe me, if tire-tread jeans, shirts and fedoras had been available through the normal retail channels, your girl would have known about it.) Yep, this guy had lovingly assembled slivers of used tread into a jersey and a hat and an ass-glorious pair of thirty by thirty-six pants—how, I couldn't even imagine. The thought that he had personally created this costume made me even hornier, and I could feel my bud twitching like a tiny, excited animal. Even as he stood magnificently at the counter in his ensemble, I could see him naked on a wooden floor, surrounded by fragrant rubber, diligently tailoring his masterpiece. I wanted to suck him and fuck him on all that rubber, in all that rubber, around all that rubber.

I decided it was time to order another espresso.

"Your clothes smell great." I couldn't believe I'd blurted that out, right at the counter. Well, yeah, maybe I could.

"Thank you."

I wasn't sure whether or not I should be surprised that *he* didn't look surprised by my abrupt compliment. Did he hear this stuff all fucking day, from tire-crazed vixens in burnt-rubber heat? I had thought this was a quiet town.

"I'm Mitch."

As always, I was fascinated by the fact that the tire rubber, which looked so black from a distance, revealed itself to be a handsome gray when viewed up close.

"Hi, Mitch. I'm Ruth. Do you mind if I feel your tread?"

He smiled. "Why not? After all, I don't have any biceps to speak of."

He bent an elbow and offered me a forearm. I ran my finger, with slow ecstasy, along one of the sensuous grooves. The soft, squishy sound of my fingertip dragging along the rubber seemed thunderous in my ears, and I could swear I felt his skin warming through the rubber, beneath my touch. My panties were so damp I was sure they'd soon start dripping like a percolator onto the black-and-white checkerboard floor.

"There are empty seats back there where I'm set up," I said, cocking my head in the direction of my knapsack and my novel and the couch I'd nearly anointed with my arousal. *Thank God,* I thought, *for cafés that are conveniently crowded in the front and attractively empty toward the back.*

"I have a thing for rubber," I confessed after he'd settled into place next to me on the couch, at my invitation. My gaze was locked on the artificial six-pack created by the texture of his industrial-strength shirt.

"You don't say," Mitch replied affably. He took a sip of his coffee, then he laughed. "I *knew* we had something in common."

I'd been so fixated on his clothes that I hadn't given enough attention to his face. Now I saw how his brown eyes glowed at me from beneath the brim of the fedora and how his smile sang boyishly from inside the confines of his Vandyke.

So I helped myself to two handfuls of tire-clad torso and kissed Mitch, hard, breathing a cocktail of rubber and after-shave. Within moments, we were giving new meaning to the term *rubberneckers.*

As our bodies heated up, I could smell the sweetness of his fresh perspiration leeching the essence of the tires. I could imagine the slick sensations he must be feeling across his skinny chest as the warm rubber suckled his skin. I was making his entire body wet, the way my own ravenous sex was wet, and the only thing I wanted in the world was to jam his cock inside me while our senses snaked together in a rubber-infused fog of pleasure.

He had somehow sewn a zipper into the front of his pants, and I was on it, with little concern for the fact that we were, technically, in a public place. I hadn't done anything this brash since my I-95 days, but I was officially a woman out of control at this point. And I wasn't hearing any complaints from Mitch.

Whenever time constraints force me to choose between eating and being eaten, I'll usually vote to have my pussy tongued till I scream. But I'd known from the moment I first saw Mitch that I wanted to snack on his dick, to lick along the length of it like my saliva was a dribble of mustard and his cock a sizzling hot dog, protruding trigonometrically from a charcoal-tinted rubber roll.

As I went down on him, it made me feel ticklish to sense the contrast between his naked flesh—so delicate yet so rigid—and the rugged lewdness of the pants. The treads looked like cartoonishly exaggerated corduroy wales, and I gripped them for stability as my head bobbed and kissed and nurtured its way up and down the pale, stiff prize. He was sensitive, and he cooed for me like a tweepop singer as I brought him closer, moment by delicious moment, to delivering a coffeeless cream into my mouth.

"Are you guys done with your drinks?"

Frankly, I was glad we'd been thrown out right after Mitch's pretty dick exploded for me, because the café was beginning to cramp my style. I wanted to sprawl naked for him on my futon, to feel him roll softly over me in his tire treads, to sense the chemistry of flesh and rubber fusing me to him and melting my entire body into Campbell's cream of cunt soup. While Mitch glanced backward into the place we'd been ejected from, I was looking forward to all of this.

I may be an unapologetically promiscuous adventurer, but it's a quaint social nicety of mine that if I bring a boy home to fuck him silly, I make a point of exchanging full names. After the café, it felt a bit anticlimactic, but a rule is a rule.

"I should tell you that my birth certificate says 'Ruth Obergard,'" I volunteered a little shyly, just as we were crossing under the local I-95 overpass.

"Mitchell Lynne," he responded, extending a hand with mock formality.

We walked on quietly. *My Michelin Man,* I thought inanely. I laughed without explaining, and he seemed to like that.

I'd been jonesing for the futon, but it was a beautiful day, so I decided to introduce Mitch to my tire swing first. He sat for me there, his cock proud as a stick shift in its glossy black condom, and I peeled down my juice-stained panties and straddled him. Under my flimsy skirt, my naked thighs rode a tarmac of cheeky rubber. I loved feeling how it was sort of hard and soft at the same time when I pressed into it.

Once I was sure our positions were stable, I let myself go wild on him. As my flesh slapped down more and more frantically, I could no longer tell where Mitch's pants ended and the tire swing began. All I knew was that rubber kissed my soft ass with every thrust of my hips. And while our combined momentum made the swing move faster than I was used to, my crazy snatch gushed onto the rubber-sheathed prick and the rubber-clothed lap. When Mitch released his come and daintily touched my clit, the little backyard spun around us faster than tractor-trailer wheels.

In my bedroom, Mitch was soft in his rubber pants. So he simply rolled over and over me, like I'd imagined, and his kind eyes watched my face as I fucked myself beneath him—relishing his texture, absorbing his smell, practically crying because I had what I craved and craved what I had. I came like a romantic—now actually sobbing with joy—and I fell asleep beneath a blanket of masculine rubber.

For all those years, I had come again and again on the interstate. Now, at last, the interstate had come home to me.

And I didn't even need a fucking car.

JUSTINE, IN LATEX

Lillian Ann Slugocki

In the beginning there was Justine.

Preternaturally meticulous Justine.

Justine in her gray skirt and matching vest, a gold pin on her blue blouse, a strand of pearls around her neck, sensible pumps in the fall and one-piece bathing suits in the summer, expensive leather handbags and gold watches. Blunt cuts and herringbone. A woman out in the world.

See Justine as she walked down a crowded street, the blue sky, like a slice of turquoise, the sun just beginning to set. See her carrying two big bags of groceries, paper not plastic, her cell phone, and her laptop slung over her right shoulder. Watch her sigh as she approached her mother's house. Note the strong jaw, the full lips, the deep wide-set eyes, the long muscular legs, the tightly constrained yet luscious breasts.

"Yes, Mother, yes. I said yes. I will be there when I get there and the longer you annoy me about how long is it going to take until I get there, the longer it's going to take. Love you, good-bye." She snapped the phone shut, gave the finger to a car that almost cut her off, then called her assistant, Amanda. "Make sure you email me the latest draft of the contracts. Make sure you notate every change in red ink, not black ink or blue ink and by the way, my coffee was cold this morning, and who is that new secretary, who sent her over, who? Who? Well, tell them to send me somebody with half a brain next time, and fire her ass."

Sometimes Justine could be a bitch.

She arrived at her mother's house, a neat suburban ranch, beige brick covered in ivy, with pink azalea bushes by the front door. Impatiently, she knocked, then knocked again. Through the octagonal window she saw Sally, her mother, wearing men's boxers, a long white T-shirt, her cat-eye glasses hanging from a white chain around her neck and black kitten-heel pumps. As if this were not enough, Sally, mother of Justine, wore bright red lipstick, and long dangly earrings. Was she always going to dress like a biker chick? Was there no hope, no redemption for this woman?

"Ma," she hollered impatiently, "answer the door, will ya? My arms are killing me."

Sally flung open the door and said, "You know what your trouble is Justine? Do you?"

"What, Ma, what is my trouble?" Justine advanced into the living room, dropped the groceries off in the kitchen, and came back.

Sally replied, "It's been ages since you've had a boyfriend."

"Stay out of my sex life."

"What sex life?"

Justine sighed and plopped down on the brown velour sofa, put her feet up on the ottoman, and congratulated herself for escaping, barely, with her life. This might've all been hers, the silk floral arrangements, the family pictures in silver-plated frames, the deep pile rug, the ratty old armchair, all the dust and detritus of suburban life. The sunlight slanted through the bay window, framed by faux silk drapes tied back with heavily tasseled gold rope. Justine shuddered. Her mother planted herself before her daughter and repeated, "What sex life?"

Justine closed her eyes, "Ma, please. Just—just don't."

"I think it's time to bring out my secret weapon."

"Ma!" Justine implored and sunk lower onto the sofa.

But it was too late. Sally was off on a mission. Justine wondered whether she could have a beer. She still had to get those reports finished by tomorrow morning, and tonight was the night she did her hair and nails. Better not, she thought sadly. Sometimes it was all too much—being the modern woman, having a career, paying the bills, putting the food on the table, bringing home the bacon. She had watched her one and only true friend, Jennifer, marry a lawyer, quit her job and now prance around seven months pregnant. What kind of life was that? Barefoot and pregnant? Where was the power, the glory? Before she could answer herself, Sally marched back into the living room cradling a box in her arms.

"What are those?" Justine asked. "Christmas decorations?"

Sally sat across from her, the box now on her lap.

"Now, darling, I know that you think I'm a middle-aged hausfrau, past my prime, but in my younger days, in the seventies, when I would go out catting, I would wear this—" And with a flourish she opened the box and pulled out latex panties and a matching bra. Bright red. Fire-engine red. Hot. They glinted obscenely in the sunlight, jarringly and shockingly out of place in this suburban landscape with its box hedges and sprinklers and girls' bicycles strewn across lawns already riddled with soccer balls and rosebushes.

In shock, Justine stood. "Mom, put those away. Okay? In fact, I forbid you to show me any more of your underwear."

Sally was insistent, "Put these underneath that stuck-up gray suit of yours and men will be falling at your feet. Trust me, a mother knows."

"How much acid did you do in the seventies?"

"I'm serious." Sally sat down next to her. "All work and no play makes Justine a very boring, uptight girl."

"I'm a woman, Mother, not a girl," Justine replied, moving away from her, "and this is not an appropriate conversation for us to be having. We should be talking about recipes and chicken and the high cost of milk. Not your"—and here her voice dropped to a deep whisper—"your rubber underwear! Furthermore, if you're prancing around in kitten heels in the middle of the day drinking beer, one may safely assume that you've recovered from your toenail surgery and can get your own groceries."

See Justine, miserable, chastened by her mother, walking ten blocks to the nearest train, the red latex underwear hidden in the bottom of her bag. It seemed as if they were burning a hole, as if they were on fire. Justine was sure that every Tom, Dick and, yes, Harry knew her shameful secret. But in point of fact, Justine knew that her mother was right. She had rejected every model of womanhood given to her—her mother's, her friends', the ridiculous women on TV, the women on the soaps and gracing the covers of the latest self-help books. Justine wanted none of that, but what she wanted and how she wanted it remained a mystery. So she took the underwear just to shut Sally up.

Back at home, deep in the dark heart of the city, in her towering glass-and-steel high-rise, she ran the water for her bath. She had ten minutes at the most, then there were the reports already stacked up on her minimalist Scandinavian desk to be done, the blue pens and the red pens neatly arrayed to the right of the stack. Stripped down and now naked, Justine pondered for a moment the red latex underwear still languishing at the bottom of her computer bag. Surely it wouldn't hurt to take them out, even though she couldn't for one instant fathom herself wearing them under any circumstances.

Tentatively, she unzipped the bag, slightly averted her head, and pulled out the panties. In the dim glow of the apartment, the red shiny fabric glistened wetly like a pair of lips. Justine dropped her towel. What was this? What was happening? Somewhere deep inside of her, she began to vibrate. Was it her heart, was it her brain, was it her pussy? None of her previous lovers had ever ignited this fire inside her. Not Fred, the junior accountant, who trembled so violently with desire he actually passed gas. Not Gus, the handyman, whose strong forearms masked a penis the size of a string bean, and who had the temerity to announce, "I don't eat pussy."

She set the panties down on the kitchen table as if they might be radioactive, but then approached them again, fingering the surprisingly silky texture, rubbing it between her thumb and forefinger. Then an image formed of her mother, decked out in her leather gear, astride a Harley, wearing these underneath—no, it was too much, too retarded, almost incestuous. She retreated quickly and had her bath. Justine luxuriated in the hot water, in the gleaming stainless-steel fixtures, the marble sink, the order and precision of her potions and oils. To her relief, the vibrating diminished, subsided, until it was barely a tremor.

She rubber herself raw with a rich Egyptian cotton towel, lush and luxurious, and sprinkled her body with baby powder and thought of how easily the panties would slide up over her ass now that it was shining clean and dusted with a light layer of talcum. *Where did that come from?* Justine looked around the room, almost expecting to see someone else, but she was alone. The voice rose up again. It would be so easy, they would slide like silk—stop. No. The year-end projections, the budget cuts, the board members all waiting, poised like chickens in a henhouse, an army of men and women wearing somber gray, decorous navy, kelly green accents, gold hoops, clucking over their imported coffee. Waiting for her, Justine, to begin the meeting, at 8:00 a.m. sharp.

See Justine as she hovered between a precipice of responsibility and desire; sweat dripping from her brow, trailing down her neck, drop by drop onto her spine; her nipples now completely erect.

See her fall.

Once again, she approached the panties splayed out like a mouth on her kitchen table. At the very least, she could wash them out, remove all traces of Sally, and try them on. What could it hurt?

See the sun as it rose on a glorious new day, the golden-hued light glittering from the sky, a slight breeze. Read closely and see that the *Farmer's Almanac* recorded it as one of the most perfect days of the century. At 7:15 a.m., Justine stood in her kitchen, wearing a coral suit, her waist cinched with a brown leather belt, three-inch platforms, pouring coffee in her ultramodern kitchen with the slate countertops and marble floors, moving as if choreographed.

At her office, at 8:00 a.m. sharp, she was focused and diligent—she double-checked the status of the boardroom, returned her emails, blithely arranged for a complex series of documents to be shipped from the London office, then consumed a leisurely breakfast of a bran muffin and half a cantaloupe at her glass-topped desk. Once finished, she surveyed her kingdom, breathed in and out, then stopped at her assistant's desk minutes before the board meeting,

"Amber, you look lovely today. Are those gold earrings?"

Amber, stunned and almost in shock, replied, "Yes, they were my mother's."

"Gorgeous, absolutely gorgeous, love the way they frame your face. So," she added, smiling, "are we ready?"

At that exact moment, the madams and misters began to somberly file into the boardroom, clearing their throats, pouring glasses of mineral water into crystal tumblers, arranging their pens and pencils, settling their rather large derrieres into the comfortable black leather chairs. They murmured hellos to each other, then settled back, as was the custom, and waited for Justine. Our Justine.

Who just might have a new trick up her sleeve.

Precisely two minutes late, again, as was the custom, Justine strode into the boardroom, but then pulled the blinds open wide so that the light, muted before, now fell into the room like the shock of cold water. Her manager looked up at her, a faint look of disapproval on his face, as if to say, this is not what we do, this is not how we behave, this is not right, in fact, this is wrong. Justine pretended not to see this, although she was not stupid and knew exactly what he was thinking.

Her cell phone rang; another look from her boss. "Not now, Mother," she murmured, then turned off the phone and turned to face her people.

"Ladies and gentlemen, good morning. I won't mince words. This year at TechNo Industries is shaping up to be very interesting, one might even say fascinating, and I don't think it's a stretch to say that you have signed on for the ride of your life."

This was the Justine her manager knew and loved, confident, poised, in control. This was why, she knew, he had promoted her to vice president, even though she was only thirty-five. She watched as he settled back in his chair, took another microbite from his cinnamon pastry and began to relax. This was her show. Yes, indeed. Everyone else began to relax as well, choosing to ignore her earlier blatant disregard for decorum. In fact, Ms. Perry from the corporate secretary's office, whose job it was to record the minutes of the meeting, stealthily stood up, and closed the blinds, just an inch or two. Justine swiftly turned on her and said, "Exactly what the fuck are you doing, Ms. Perry?" The crowd gasped. Had Justine lost her mind?

Her manager dropped his pastry, crumbs littering his dark wool suit, his jaw agape.

"Justine," he managed to say, almost choking, "What on earth—"

But before he could get the words out of his mouth, Justine leapt onto a conference chair, then, unbelievably, onto the oak table, kicking the piles of papers with her stilettos, the red latex underwear clinging to her hips, her thighs, her breasts, like silk, but more insistent, like a jealous lover, like perfume. She was a superpower, woman times ten, perhaps twenty, dead center on the conference table. She reached down for her briefcase, opened it, took out a whip, and snapped it smartly across the table. "The fourth quarter will be great. We will see a fifteen percent increase in profits."

Snap! She cracked the whip again. "Our sales are through the roof, once again, and you have me to thank for the profit that lines the pockets of your designer suits." The whip coiled through the air and several people moved away in horror. "You are all about to become very, very rich," she proclaimed as it landed, *snap*, on the oak table. "So wipe those looks off your faces, before I do it for you. But that's not all ladies and gentlemen, that is not all—"

Slowly, provocatively, she began to strip, unbuttoning her coral silk jacket, flinging it off; her fingers sliding down the zipper of her skintight skirt, then slowly, slowly wriggling her hips till it lay in a bright tangle at her feet; then her camisole came off, and her stockings, until she had revealed the secret of her power, the hidden glamour of her audacity, Mama's red latex underwear, fire-engine red, hot as hellfire.

"These are the projections and the numbers and the profit that will make you come and come again."

In the beginning was Justine, who, once upon a time, strutted across a boardroom table, before the shocked faces of her audience, in all her glory, all eyes on her rubber-encased buttocks, her ample breasts now sheathed in bright red. She was predatory, outrageous, cracking her whip and laughing. No one said a word. But one by one, beginning with her manager, they all began to smile. Tentatively at first, but then, by God, they really began to enjoy the show. Some even began to clap. Amber brought in her iPod, hooked it up to the speakers, turned it up, then turned it up again, until music blasted throughout the room, until everyone was dancing. Some of them even joined Justine on the table.

After the meeting, Justine, still half-naked, cornered her manager in his office.

"I need you to fuck me," she ordered.

"I c-can't," he stuttered.

"Why not?" she demanded.

"I have erectile d-d—I can't get it up. I'm fifty-five, for God's sake, and the rules clearly state that I cannot take advantage of you—" he gasped, stepping back from her.

Cracking her whip inches from his face, she said, "Do I look like someone you could take advantage of?"

"No," he replied, almost smiling. "Not in the least."

"Then do as I say," she commanded, her voice dropping an octave, her moist hands sliding up and down the fire-engine red rubber underwear, now glistening with sweat, glowing under the fluorescent lights as if they were alive, an animal presence, glued to every inch of her body, pulsating. She cracked her whip again, wrapping the braided leather around his waist, gently pulling him toward her.

"Come here, little boy, Mama's not going to hurt you."

When he was inches from her face, she grabbed his right hand and ran it up and down the length and breadth of her body, paying special attention to her breasts and nipples, then did the same to him. After a few moments, he raggedly said, "Isn't this sexual harassment?" His cock hardened beneath her touch.

"You better believe it," she replied. "And I want you to harass this little section, right here," and she guided his hand to her pussy as she pulled aside her rubber panties. His index finger snaked up inside, finding her glistening and dripping wet. She grabbed his cock, whispered in his ear, "You feel pretty functional to me." She loosened her hold on him, stepped back a few inches, and pulled up the bra, exposing her breasts, her nipples now as red as cut roses. She observed his erection—magnificent.

"I never thought you were attracted to me," he said, now brazenly massaging his cock.

"I'm not," Justine announced. "This is a one-time deal."

Justine fucked her manager on his conference table, her legs waving wildly in the air for all the world to see, then she sat on his face as he lay spread-eagled on the beige carpet. Finally, finally, Justine could feel the heat building up inside of her, vibrating like a strobe light, flickering faster and faster, the fire-engine brassiere still clinging to her, transforming her. For one brief instant she blacked out, a constellation of stars appeared, and then came the orgasm. Office workers two floors above and two floors below phoned in a possible earthquake and sure enough, *something* registered 2.5 on the Richter scale. But this could be urban legend. Only Justine knows the truth.

After five years of making full use of them, and many adventures and promotions, Justine put away her rubber underwear with a silent prayer of thanks to Sally. But only temporarily. After all, she was five months pregnant, and someday her daughter might need them.

BATHING BEAUTY

Andrea Dale

It all started because Paul's mother was an Esther Williams fan.

He grew up watching the sleek swimmer, respectful of and fascinated by strong, independent, creative women.

And rubber bathing caps.

I didn't actually learn this about him until we found an old poster of Esther in an antiques-and-collectibles shop at the shore. It had a funky and eclectic décor, and I thought the poster was neat, too, so we bought it and had it framed and hung it on our sunporch, which had something of a nautical theme already.

It wasn't until I came home early from shopping with the girls one day and found Paul masturbating to the poster that I suspected that anything was up.

I wasn't upset or even concerned. We had a healthy sex life, and, hey, sometimes a guy (and even a girl) has to take matters into his own hands. In fact, the sight of him sitting there, cock red and slick in his fist, made me feel frisky enough to dive in and help out.

I knelt between his legs and took the hot, hard length of him into my mouth.

He'd been at it long enough that his own sweet precome mingled with the mostly flavorless lubricant he'd used. I flicked my tongue against the little hole to coax out more of the sweet liquid. He whispered, "Oh, yeah," and caressed my hair, not quite pulling me down harder on him, but encouraging me to continue at will.

It wasn't long before I felt his balls tense and heard his breathing catch, and I knew he was on the edge. My pussy tingled in empathetic response (knowing too that he'd return the favor) as I coaxed out his pleasure. I looked up at him as he came, and saw his eyes were wide, and fixed on the poster.

I asked him about it later, when we were in bed, and he confessed everything like a naughty schoolboy who always knew—and even half-hoped—that his secret would be discovered.

Esther had consumed his boyhood fantasies, featured heavily in his adolescent longings. His first wet dream had been of her (and we both laughed at the pun in that). Finally, out of erotic desperation, he'd stolen his mother's rubber bathing cap. It was lime green, he said, with big flowers sprouting off it. Hideous but compelling.

He knew he couldn't give it back to her afterward, so he said the dog had chewed it up. He kept it hidden under his mattress for years, brought out only in the dead of night.

Paul was a little hesitant as he told me the story, watching for my reaction, having to be coaxed to tell all the details. We'd been happily experimental when it came to sex, but he'd worried that this was a little farther over the edge than I'd be interested in. I knew, too, that he'd feared tainting the adolescent fantasy. I reassured him, and in the end he said he was glad to be able to tell me.

What he didn't know is that I was already mentally plotting a nice, sticky, fun birthday surprise for him.

Luckily, I had time to prepare, because it took me a while to find exactly what I needed. I wasn't even sure it existed. But it did: a retro waterskiing show, the kind with people stacked in a pyramid, like in the "Vacation" video by the Go-Go's.

Best part was, they wore bathing caps.

Not rubber ones, alas, but close enough for my purposes and, I hoped, Paul's desires. From afar, it wouldn't really be easy to tell what the elaborate headdresses were made of. It was the show that counted.

Plus there'd be synchronized swimming. And proper bathing caps or no, that had to count for something. It was an Esther Williams fan's dream come true.

When Paul woke on his birthday morning, I greeted him with a kiss, a cappuccino, a bagel with cream cheese and lox, and a card that told him he was going to have a special day.

Lunch was a lovely meal at a prime seafood restaurant at the shore, and then we were off to the show.

Paul had a mix of mild confusion and burgeoning lust on his face when he realized what we were about to see. I snuggled up against him and breathed into his ear, "This is your special day, honey. Enjoy."

He enjoyed, all right. More than once I saw him adjust himself, and for a while he even laid his program over his lap to ensure innocent bystanders weren't treated to an eyeful. I was tempted to bring him off right there at the show, but the bleachers weren't exactly set up for any modicum of privacy, and it would kind of spoil the occasion if we got arrested for public indecency.

I had other, better plans.

In the parking lot, he backed me up against the car and kissed me, his tongue darting into my mouth in a way that always makes me think only of how that would feel on my clit (and I always knew that pleasure would be forthcoming). He pressed his hips against mine, and I felt the outline of his hard cock against my mound.

"Thank you, sweetheart," he said when we broke for air. "That *was* special."

"Oh, we're not through yet," I said, unable to keep the teasing glee from my voice. "This was just...foreplay."

I swear I felt his cock twitch against me. We decided I should be the one to drive home, just to be safe.

It wasn't long before I had Paul naked and stretched out on our bed, his cock at half-mast, pulsing toward full erection as he imagined what erotic surprises I might have in store for him.

He'd been a competitive swimmer in high school and college, and had the body for it: long and lean with sleek, seal-like muscles, broad shoulders and narrow hips, and he was mostly hairless, so he hadn't had to shave his chest and legs like some of his teammates. Indeed, I'd always been hot for the way he looked in a Speedo, the shiny Lycra outlining the taut dimples in his hips and the heavy soft package of his penis and balls cupped in the front.

I didn't think I had a rubber fetish myself, but I found myself wondering how his groin would look encased in rubber—deep royal blue, to bring out his eyes.

As if I'd be looking at his eyes.

We'd played with cock rings before—simple leather adjustable ones—so I figured a slightly stretchy rubber one wouldn't be too much of a step up. I rolled it down Paul's cock, gently tucked it behind his balls. Now he was fully hard, his cock like velvet-covered steel in my hands.

He reached for me, nuzzling my breasts before grazing his teeth across my nipples, just the way I like it. I'd been wet all day, really, just imagining how this would go, and now a fresh wave of desire shimmered through me, from nipples to clit. I wanted more.

That's when I pulled out the bathing cap.

Yep, I'd found one of those old rubber ones. It wasn't lime green, unfortunately, but white, with a couple of red and blue flowers on one side that gave it the look of a cloche hat from the 1920s.

Paul sucked in his breath when he saw it. With a deliberately lewd grin, I sprawled back on the bed and stretched it across my pussy. "Dive in," I suggested.

He didn't need further encouragement. He rarely did, but this time he was like a man possessed, breathing in the rubbery smell as he found my clit.

It wasn't long before I needed more, though. The material was just too thick for me to get full sensation—and I needed it right now. I pulled the cap away, and he paused, just for a moment, to turn it over and run his tongue along the side that had been against me, tasting my juices coating the rubber. His eyes were closed, his face worshipful. Then he turned back to me, and he gave me the same adoring attention.

I held the cap across his neck and used it to pull him closer as my thighs started to tremble. My orgasm wasn't long in coming, but I could feel every second, every degree of it as the erotic sensations pooled down below. My legs and stomach tightened, and then the flick of Paul's tongue against me finally pushed me over the edge.

It took me a moment to recover, but when I did, it was time to focus on him.

To my amazement—and, I'll confess, delight—I almost sent

Paul over the edge when I rubbed the bathing cap across his nipples. I knew he was sensitive there, but the feel of the rubber heightened things exponentially. I expect the cock ring was the only thing that kept him from coming from the nipple play alone.

Well. He was close, and I wanted to bring him off so much my clit was tingling again in anticipation. I trailed the cap across his balls, watching as they jumped, listening to breath hissing between his teeth.

I slipped my hand into the cap and drizzled rubber-friendly lube across it, and then, using it almost like a mitten, wrapped it and my fingers around his steely cock.

He cried out my name, his hips rising off the bed. Just a few tight strokes, and he was pulsing and twitching, his come mingling with the lube, the musky scent mingling with the rubber smell, and I think I had a sympathetic miniclimax just from watching him and hearing him.

You'd think that would be enough. But we played long into the night. I don't know—I didn't think rubber was my thing. Still, there's this bra-and-panty set I've found online, in a jaunty red, that I've got my eye on...

IN THE MIDDLE

Jessica Lennox

There is a hazard to becoming friends with two people who are involved with each other. If by some stroke of bad luck the relationship ends, you end up in the middle.

There is an unspoken rule that you will no longer invite both halves of said broken-up couple to any gathering. Even worse, one half of said broken-up couple will claim that you were his or her friend first, which equates to "I don't want you talking to my ex anymore." Of course, at the forefront of unspoken rules is this one: If you are a woman, you will remain friends with the female half of the broken-up couple. Anything to the contrary is met with great suspicion among friends, coworkers, neighbors and especially the ex.

I can't really say that Julie and Mark were close friends of mine—we met at a fundraiser and ended up joining the organization that was hosting the event. We ran into each other a few times, then started socializing together more and more as time went on. Eventually we became acquaintances, and I suppose some semblance of "friends."

When I first met them, Julie seemed rather unapproachable, but Mark was extremely friendly. I suspected Julie might not appreciate Mark's attention toward me, but once she realized I wasn't a threat, she dropped her guard and allowed our friendship to bloom. Still, I always made sure to keep my boundaries firmly in place so as not to cause any misunderstandings.

I have to admit, on more than one occasion I wondered what they looked like in bed together—they're both gorgeous, and I'd gotten a few hints here and there that they might be into something more than just plain, vanilla sex. I never felt it was appropriate to delve into that topic, but every so often, one of them would make a quick comment before moving on to the next subject.

I had gotten used to seeing them at least once every week or two, so when I didn't hear from either one of them for almost three weeks, and neither showed up for our fundraising group, I started to wonder if everything was okay. Finally, I emailed Julie just to say hi, and hoped she'd offer some insight. I didn't want to be nosy, so I didn't come right out and ask, but she answered by telling me that she and Mark were taking a break, and she was having a hard time with it. She said things were friendly but strained. I silently and selfishly hoped they would work it out because I wasn't ready to go through another "couple breakup." The next thought to follow was, which one of them would flip out on me and tell me not to talk to the other if indeed they did break up?

I told Julie to call me if she needed or wanted company and left it up to her to contact me at her leisure. I didn't attempt to contact Mark, even though I had his email address. Although I was certain Julie trusted me, I didn't want to cause any further problems.

The following week, Julie phoned and said she and Mark were going to a movie, and asked if I'd come along, just so things weren't weird. I thought that in itself was weird, but I agreed to go for her sake.

I met them outside the theater and exchanged awkward hellos with each of them, along with awkward hugs and strained smiles. Once inside, Julie chose the seats and stepped into the row first, then Mark motioned for me to go next. Great, I was going to be in the middle. Could it get any weirder than this?

Happily, we didn't have to wait long before the previews started, and I could escape the awkwardness and just concentrate on the movie. I looked around as the lights started to dim. The theater was almost completely empty. Apparently only a handful of people besides us were interested in seeing a subtitled French film.

I tried to relax and forget that I was in the middle of two obviously stressed-out, anxious people. After a few minutes, I realized Mark's leg was resting lightly against mine. I tried to ignore it and not make anything out of it. Surely it wasn't on purpose; he was probably just relaxed and didn't even notice it. As I tried to forget about it and concentrate on the movie, I felt his leg press against mine with unmistakable certainty. I didn't move; I didn't look at him; I kept my body stiff and rigid wondering what in the hell he was doing, especially considering his girlfriend was sitting directly beside me, break or no break. I tried to sneak a peek at Julie to see if she had noticed anything out of the ordinary, but she seemed to be caught up in the movie. I let out a sigh of relief, louder than I meant to, and felt Julie shift in her seat.

Then I felt Mark's arm brush against mine as he placed his hand on his thigh. His fingertips were lightly touching my leg where it rested against his. Now I was getting a little freaked out. Was he doing this on purpose? How far did he intend to go? And would I let him? I know—it's a complete breach of friendship, but I hadn't had sex in a really long time, and my libido was suddenly overriding my common sense.

I was so caught up in what was going on with Mark, I wasn't even paying attention to the movie, but when I finally focused on the screen, I saw a nude woman standing on a pedestal in an art studio while someone (presumably an artist) painted her with thick, bright-colored paint.

Julie leaned toward me and whispered in a sexy voice, "Doesn't that look fun?"

"Mmm-hmmm," I mumbled as I felt Mark's hand caress the side of my leg.

"She's got a perfect body for that," Julie whispered.

"Yeah," I sighed in agreement.

The woman did have a splendid figure, and I found myself getting aroused as the painter in the film paid special attention to her breasts. I wondered what any of this had to do with the context of the overall plot, but I was starting not to care as the painter moved downward toward the woman's sex.

"Spread your legs," the painter onscreen said. I only knew this because of the subtitles.

I moaned as the painter started to slather the woman's pussy with bright blue.

Julie whispered, "She's gorgeous, isn't she?" and I nodded in agreement as the woman onscreen spread her legs.

"What is...?" I started to ask, confused when the paint on her body seemed to stretch.

Julie leaned over and whispered in my ear, "It's liquid latex. Like rubber. It's really sexy, and fun to play with. I'd like to try it on you sometime. You know, just to show you."

I reluctantly tore my attention from the screen so I could look

Julie square in the eye. When I did that, she glanced down and noticed Mark's hand touching my leg.

I instantly panicked, thinking we were soon going to be in the middle of an all-out catfight, but instead, she looked back at me and smiled. As my expression went from guilty to confused, she again leaned toward me and whispered in my ear, "It's okay, Jacqueline, I know you're attracted to him. I also know you're conflicted about it. I want to tell you it's okay, you can fuck him. But only if you let me watch."

I snapped my head back to look at her again. Had I heard her right? She was okay with me fucking her boyfriend?!

I had my answer when she reached across my lap, grabbed Mark's hand, and placed it between my legs. Not only did the pressure on my pussy feel good, but the forbidden aspect of it all was making me really hot.

Suddenly my head cleared and I said out loud, "I don't want to do this here. Let's go."

I stood up and Julie and Mark looked at each other, then also stood up. We filed out of the theater and headed into the parking lot. Once we were in Mark's car, nobody said a word. Finally Julie turned around in her seat and said, "Okay, I can't stand the silence. I have to confess, this was sort of a setup. We're not on a break anymore, but we both agreed we need to spice things up a bit, and that's what led to all of this. I know it was a bit manipulative, but I didn't want to come right out and ask you. I wanted to have a chance to feel you out, so to speak. I hope you're not upset."

I paused for a few moments to absorb what she'd said, then responded, "I'm not upset, I'm concerned. I don't want this to change our friendship."

"Well, I can't promise it won't," Julie said, "but I think we're all mature enough and trust each other enough to remain friends, perhaps even become better friends."

As we pulled up to their house, Julie asked, "Are we all in agreement then?"

I looked at her and smiled, then said, "Yes and no, but yes."

We all laughed. Mark still hadn't said anything, so I finally asked him, "Are you okay with this?"

He looked at me in the rearview mirror and said, "Hell, yeah. I'm more than okay with it," then winked at me.

When we were inside their house, Julie asked Mark to get us all a drink, then led me downstairs to the basement. I was slightly amused when I realized the area she had led me to looked very much like the art studio in the movie we had just been watching. There was an area of the room where plastic was spread out over the floor along with a large piece of eggshell foam, like the kind you'd place over a futon frame. On the table nearby were several cans stacked in a neat pile and some neatly folded washcloths.

Julie let me take it all in, then turned to me. "I meant what I said. I'd like to try the latex on you. That is, if you'll let me."

"I'd like that. I'm always up for trying something new," I said with seductive smile.

Julie grinned, then said, "I'll paint you, then watch as Mark peels it off and fucks you."

When she said that, my nipples got hard and I started to fidget. "Okay. Now what?"

"Take off your clothes."

I didn't need her to tell me twice. I quickly removed everything and stood there naked under her watchful eye. Julie told me to place everything on the chair and then stand on the plastic sheet that had been laid out.

"Nervous?" she asked.

"A little. I mean, I'm not a prude, but this is a new experience, which makes it a little scary. But in a fun way," I quickly added.

"Good. First I have to apply a moisturizer," she said, squeezing the lotion into her palm. As soon as she made contact with my skin, I jumped. "Sorry, I know it's cold," she said.

I laughed at my own nervousness, but soon found myself concentrating on how good her hands were making me feel. She had a sensual stroke that started at my neck and wandered down toward my breasts. My nipples were already hard, and now that she was making her way toward my pussy, my clit was starting to throb.

"Looks like things are progressing down here," Mark said as he entered the room, startling me out of my reverie.

"Yes, she's being a very good girl," Julie replied.

Mark put three glasses of wine on the table, then settled into one of the comfortable chairs. I noticed he had a hard-on under his jeans.

"Okay, that part's done," Julie said. "Now for the fun stuff." I watched as she opened one of the jars on the table. "You don't have any allergies to latex, do you?"

"No," I answered, wondering if anyone had ever done this who did have an allergy.

"Now, stay as still as possible, otherwise the latex can rip or stretch and won't set well. It needs to set before we can have fun with it."

"Okay," I said, bracing myself.

"No, no, don't stiffen up. Just relax, but stay still."

I took a deep breath, then exhaled and relaxed.

"This might be a little cold as I apply it, but it'll warm up, so just try to relax. Let's start with some crimson."

As she dipped her hand into the can and scooped the thick liquid onto my skin, my gaze drifted toward Mark. He was intently watching Julie as she basted my body, and I was hyper-aware that he was lustfully staring at my breasts. I continued to watch him and when he looked up and saw me, he let his hand wander downward until he was touching the bulge in his jeans. I took a deep breath and remembered to relax as Julie continued her task. It seemed to be taking a long time, and I was starting to feel rather impatient. I mean, it was cool to experience something new, but I wanted to get down to the good stuff!

"Spread your legs for me a little," Julie directed me in a soft voice.

I moved my feet apart a bit and then a little more as she spread the thick liquid over my hips and groin area. Then she grabbed another can and said, "Let's try the Starlight Blue."

I watched as she wiped her hand with one of the washcloths, then peeled off a few red gobs from her arm. "You're really wet, so I'm going to wipe you off, okay?"

I turned three shades of red, then nodded and tried to think of anything that would get my mind off her fingers probing my pussy with the washcloth. I knew I'd be wet again in seconds and there was no way of keeping it from happening. I was really starting to get off on this, and the sexual energy coming from both her and Mark was only exacerbating the situation.

I moaned, and said, "That feels good."

She just looked up and smiled at me while continuing her ministrations. I looked over at Mark and noticed he had now graduated to squeezing his cock through his jeans. I couldn't wait to get hold of it and wondered how long the latex would take to set.

Finally, Julie dropped the washcloth and dipped her hand into the blue latex. As she applied it to my smooth lips, I let out a moan and was silently thankful there was no hair down there to contend with. She continued to apply it, moving on to my legs and all the way down to my feet. When the tops of my feet were covered, she said, "Okay, we're done. Normally I would do the back, too, but it takes a while to dry, and I don't think I can wait that long. I bet you're pretty anxious to get things started, too, aren't you?"

"Yes," I whimpered in desperation.

As if on cue, Mark stood up and started taking his clothes off while Julie and I both watched. When he was completely naked, he walked over to me and tested the firmness of the latex by pressing it with his fingertip.

"Just a few more minutes."

"In the meantime," Julie said, "I'll make sure he's ready to fuck you, Jacqueline." And with that, she took his already hard cock halfway into her mouth, working the base of it with her hand as her mouth worked up and down the shaft. I whimpered in frustration. I wanted to play, too!

After a few minutes, Julie stopped, then turned toward me and pressed her fingertips against the latex on my stomach. "She's ready," she announced. *Hallelujah!* I thought.

"Do you mind if I play, too, Jacqueline? I know I said I only wanted to watch, but I'm really turned on."

"No, I don't mind. I want you to."

"Delightful," she said, as she leaned forward and licked my pussy through the latex cover.

"Oh, God, that feels good," I whispered as she expertly tongued my clit and engorged lips.

"You look so fucking sexy like this," she said.

I watched her tongue trace the outline of my pussy before grabbing the latex with her teeth and ripping a hole through it. She took my clit between her lips and sucked gently, stopping every once in a while to kiss and bite it. I got the distinct feeling this wasn't the first time she'd done this. How many times had she and Mark invited a friend over to play?

Her hands wandered all over my body, pulling the latex

away, ripping holes in it. Her moans mixed with mine and it felt strangely erotic—almost like skin coming off, and the sudden exposure to the air made my nerves sing.

All this time Mark had been watching and stroking his cock, but now he moved in closer and started teasing my nipples with his fingertips. I wanted him to suck them, or bite them, anything! But he continued to slowly tease them through the latex barrier.

"Please fuck me," I moaned.

"Yes, Mark, I think it's time," Julie said. "She's been very patient."

"Yes, she has," Mark said, covering the foam mattress with a plastic sheet. "Lie down. I'm going to fuck you now."

Sweet Jesus, finally! I thought.

Now that I was moving around, I could feel the latex stretching and pulling, but in a very sensual way. I could see why Julie liked playing with this stuff.

Mark got between my knees and put his finger into one of the holes Julie had ripped with her teeth. As his fingers made contact with my pussy, I arched upward, desperate for more contact. I gasped when I felt cool air rush in as he ripped the opening in the latex even wider. In one smooth motion he leaned forward and pushed his cock all the way inside me. As he slowly fucked me, Julie started to peel the latex from my skin, licking and sometimes biting her way through and around it. When she peeled it from my breasts, my nipples were harder than I'd ever seen them, and she took one in her mouth while fingering the other.

I was in absolute heaven. I'd had a threesome before, and I'd even been with women before, but this definitely brought things to a new height. The kink aspect of it, the experimentation factor, the new sensations—it was all so delicious.

Julie had succeeded in peeling about half of the latex from

my torso and was now sliding her fingers downward between me and Mark to manipulate my clit.

"Wait," Mark said, and pulled out. I cried out, but realized we were just changing positions as he turned me on my side, then got behind me. Julie had been fully clothed all this time, but finally she quickly removed her clothes and lay next to me, face-to-face. Now I was sandwiched in between them as Mark entered me from behind and Julie moved down to suck on my nipple and squeeze my clit with her fingers.

It wasn't long before I gasped, "I'm coming," then came so hard I thought I was going to pass out. Mark followed suit, gritting his teeth and groaning as he pounded into me, using an arm around both me and Julie as an anchor. After a few strokes, he collapsed and lay quiet, his cock still resting inside of me.

Julie smiled at me and said, "Well, was it everything you thought it would be?"

"Jesus, yes. Everything and more," I said, enthusiastic but exhausted.

"Good. Now how about switching places and letting me be in the middle?"

LICK OF PAIN

Crystal Barela

Smooth red vinyl slipped in my saliva, but I caught the thin rubber firmly between my teeth. My eyes traveled the length of Sylvia's body from where I knelt at her feet on the newly waxed white linoleum floor. The curved walls were white as well, made even more brilliant by the fluorescent lights above us. A tire-colored length of hose secured my hands in front of me in an uncomfortably tight knot. The flesh of my upper hands swelled past the binding, flushed pussy pink.

A cocoon of shiny red brilliance covered Sylvia from ankle to chin. The latex was thin enough for me to see the belt and buckles of her strap-on. Two perfectly round holes were cut into the bodice of the dress and there her turgid nipples were made burgundy where they pressed through the openings. She looked sticky, like a giant wet lollipop. I swallowed hard, hoping my mouth was worthy of the task, that I could wrap my tongue around her body and slurp Sylvia between my plump lips, suck her from head to toe all at once.

The taste of rubber would coat my insides like a balm.

The flavor is what got me wet between my thighs. Not the tang of Sylvia's skin, but the bitter manufactured texture of the silicone that incased her luscious body.

Sylvia wanted me to use my teeth to peel the covering from her skin. She was tall, close to six feet in her stiletto-heeled platforms. From where I lay prostrate in adoration, the lights above us highlighted every curve and hollow, every nip and tuck, every beautiful inch of flesh and muscle that lay beneath the rubber's embrace. My eyes focused on the rubber bulge covering her bush. My mouth watered.

"What are you waiting for, Nadine?" Sylvia asked. I felt the rubber switch in her hand flick my bare ass in warning. I wore no clothes and my hair was pulled on top of my head in a tight bun.

My mouth tugged the latex carefully. I must not damage the garment. Sylvia would not be happy. The first few inches would have been easy—the dress was loose at the ankles—but Sylvia had spread her feet wide so that the rubber was pulled taut like a drum between the V of her legs.

I nudged upward with my lips and teeth. My cheek pressed against the smooth slickness, tempted to nuzzle, wanting to lick. And then the dress gave a millimeter, and another. I climbed Sylvia's calf, revealing a beautifully sinewed length of lower leg. The dress was new and her skin carried the flavor of the silicone's powdery sweet perfume. The scent invaded my nostrils, clogged my senses.

My tongue poked free and slipped between skin and rubber.

Instantly, the riding crop slapped my ass. The sting sent volts of electricity to my cunt, causing me to jerk away from her. Sylvia's rubber-sheathed hand swooped down and yanked hold of the bun at the back of my neck. Pins pinged to the floor and my long blonde hair fell around my shoulders. She used my hair to tear me from my knees and force me to eye level. Her dark brown eyes had blackened in color with her anger.

"Lick me again without permission and I will bloody your ass with my whip!" Sylvia said, the tone of her voice telling me she would like nothing better. The twitch of my pussy told me the same.

The slash of her riding crop was not as frightening as she thought, but pain was pain and I did not relish the angry swipe of her rubber switch on my ass. She let go and I bruised my knees when they hit the linoleum floor. I barely caught myself from falling over. I took a couple of steadying breaths and felt the riding crop beneath my chin. Sylvia directed my head back to the hem of her dress.

My teeth and lips took a firm bite of her dress and shimmied the flexible fabric to her knees. Sylvia took a purposeful step out, widening her stance, thus tightening the rubber dress. I tugged with my teeth. Nothing moved.

The riding crop was caressing my asscheeks with gentle encouraging taps.

"My last girl would have had me naked by now," Sylvia said.

Anger flushed my cheeks. I pushed hard with my forehead, but I was sweating and my face slid against the slippery silicone.

"You're an embarrassment," Sylvia said. She brought the riding crop down hard and I made a sound of denial. My ragged breath fogged the latex.

The narrow strip of air between the flaps of silicone between her knees gave me a clear, unfettered view of her huge rubber cock.

It was red, veined, beautiful new rubber. I squeezed my thighs tightly together.

Sylvia was hooked up, jacked up. She brought the switch down again.

Desperate, I forced the roughness of my hair against the latex. It inched a millimeter, then another. Static ignited my hair. I could feel the blonde strands encircle Sylvia, wind their way around her thighs and hips.

I wiggled my shoulders between her legs. My head was pushing, my teeth tugging. Her dress was no longer an erotic lure but a barrier keeping me from tasting her rubber dick.

The riding crop now fell with a steady blaze of pain, my ass on fire with it. Sylvia was laughing, enjoying my frustration.

"You desperate, dirty girl."

My head and teeth made their way to the dick bulge, but I could not pull the rubber dress over the great protuberance. It was too long and the layers of latex were now bunched up beneath the great strap-on dick I wanted to taste. I was panting with my desire; my thighs were slippery with pussy juice.

Sylvia's gloved fingers wound through my hair and she set me away from her, forcing my tender reddened asscheeks onto my calves. I moaned low in my throat and realized I was crying.

"Is this what you want, kitten?" she asked, gesturing to her midsection.

"Please," I begged. My gaze worshipped her rubber stiffy.

She took her free hand and forced the tight dress up. The cock strained, pulling upward with the dress, seeming to grow and pulse with each movement of the shiny fabric.

"Keep your mouth shut, girl," Sylvia said.

And then the great thing was free. A ruler's length of thick rubber dick slapped me hard on the face. I rubbed my cheek against the red veined beauty, pressed my forehead to its bulbous tip. My eyelashes fluttered around the length, my eyelids receiving poking kisses.

My mouth was watering. Saliva was pooling. This was a new hard-on, straight from the package. The scent was a pussy wetter: harsh, manufactured lust. My insides were like goo. My appetite ignited. I must taste. I must sample this delicacy.

My lips parted and my stomach quaked. Sylvia yanked my hair and my head snapped back away from my prize.

"Do you think you deserve a nibble, my nasty, naughty girl?" she asked. Sylvia took the thick knob of her dick in her other hand and pressed the rubber against my face. My nostrils flared. The smell was driving me insane. I wanted her to fuck my mouth, to choke me with the great rubber phallus. My tongue parted my lips.

"Nadine! You do not listen!" Sylvia pushed me away from her and I fell to my elbows. "Do not move!"

I dutifully stared at the floor in front of me, trying not to sob with disappointment. Now I would not get to suck her rubber cock. Why did I not have patience? Sylvia kicked my legs apart and rubbed the end of the cock between my thighs from behind.

"You nasty, wet girl!" she said, mopping the end of her rubber cock with my slick desire. My cunt was pulsing, wanting her rubber meat, but I wanted to taste it more. Sylvia slid through my dripping pussy and twisted her dick against my fuck-hole. She would stretch me. She would hurt me.

Sylvia was angry. You would expect her to ram me with her rubber cock, but she did not. She pressed slowly. She pushed the head against my eager pussy with deliberate calm. Sylvia knew me, knew that if I could not suck her cock, I wanted her to fuck me into the floor. So she slid into me just as slowly as I had worked the dress up her body, one millimeter at a time.

The rim of my hole strained, and I could hear the soft slurp as I took her in. Inch one, inch two, six inches, eight. And then I was too full. I could feel her thick tool on the other side of my body. I shook my head and tried to move away. She would not fit.

"Be still," Sylvia said, her voice calm. I froze. She placed a gloved hand on my hip and began to caress my skin in slow, soothing circles. Her rubber dick pressed forward.

There was nowhere for the dildo to go, I thought. Sylvia slid her arm around my body and her slippery rubber fingertips embraced my clit. She squeezed the rigid nubbin and began to milk me. Swirl and squeeze. Swirl and squeeze. My insides dripped with moisture with each pass of her hand, and Sylvia sank her fat cock home, bare thighs to my welted ass.

Sylvia swiveled her hips and I cried out. The hurting pleasure was nearly too much. She fucked me slow, with long, agonizing strokes. My clit was a hard knot of unspent desire. The wet sound of her rubber dick working my taut hole was agonizing. I needed the taste of rubber. That was the only way I would come, the only thing that would get me off.

Sylvia's hips began to move faster, jabbing my insides with intense little thrusts. Her thighs stung my ass and she reached around and twisted my breasts in her hands, latex-shrouded nails digging into my flesh. She came in a wave, undulating on my back, riding me into the floor, before she was still.

No! my mind screamed. The ache in my clit was a physical pain. I rested my forehead against my bound wrists. My breath was coming in sharp gasps. My tongue was thick and dry, aching nearly as much as my pussy.

Sylvia pulled her dick free and the acrid scent of sex and rubber hung in the air. I could feel the wet length of silicone against the back of my ass like a broken promise. She stood, and I could hear her adjusting her outfit, the squeak of her rubber-tipped fingers against the latex dress.

"Beautiful." The click of Sylvia's stilettos echoed in the room.

"Filthy." Sylvia walked to my right, past my head. "Girl." She came to a stop just in front of me.

I looked up. Sylvia stood as she had when we began the evening. She bent closer to me, her breasts moving subtly beneath her dress. Her exposed nipples became even darker. Gravity pulled the blood into the beautiful berry-shaped teat. Ripe. Ready to be picked.

Sylvia pressed her tacky fingers to my lips. They smelt of sticky clit and warm rubber. Rubber that had been in my pussy only minutes ago. The ache grew.

My eyes were pleading with Sylvia. Please!

"Lick," she said.

My tongue swiped her fingers and I began to shudder. Pussy-flavored latex. My favorite. I sucked two knuckles into my mouth and my cunt vibrated. Three fingers, four. I could have swallowed her hand, her wrist, her forearm, her elbow.

Sylvia was like candy, a beautiful gift from Wonka. I imagined gorging my insides, her body slurped whole and perfect down my throat. Her latex-encased figure would swim through my veins like a toxin. I shook.

My eyes were open, taking in the shiny red length of her forearm. The riding crop was on my ass again, slapping hard. The sound of my bruised flesh echoed in the room. The switch slid center and rode the crack of my ass down. Slick, thin rubber met my pubis.

I wanted to come. My eyes caught Sylvia's and begged for permission. With a twist of her wrists and a nod of her head, I came in a puddle of desire.

Rubber and sex had set me free.

HOW TO LIVEN UP A BORING PARTY

Teresa Noelle Roberts

Cecily fidgeted with her empty champagne flute, vaguely aware that Laine Evans was talking. Something about the school budget—or was it the other woman's departmental budget? Or the state budget?

She made what she hoped was an appropriately noncommittal "go on" noise, but she'd lost track of the conversation about ten pussy-twitches back.

Wetness.

That was what Cecily was focused on now. She could feel juices and sweat pooling in her rubber panties, making them slippery enough to stroke against her lips and clit whenever she moved. It was a warm evening, and she was sweating inside her rubber bra as well.

Under other circumstances she'd have found the sensation unpleasant, like being stuck in a damp wetsuit on a warm day.

But a wetsuit wouldn't come with a built-in rubber dildo.

Filling her.

Stretching her.

Making her aware of what a slut she was every time she took a step, every time she shifted in place.

It had made the car ride over to Gary and Jessi Ransome's house delightful torture. Every bump in the road had jarred her, pressed the dildo against her cervix, sent wavelets of sensation rippling through her body. And even when they were on the highway, she couldn't help being aware that she was wearing rubber underwear—cobalt blue with black accents—under her chocolate-brown silk Ann Taylor dress, on the way to a party thrown by one of Adam's coworkers and his wife.

She and Adam had played dress-up before: silk, lace, leather (the latter for both of them). And this was far from the first time he had convinced her to wear something completely outrageous—or nothing at all—under an ordinary outfit, to liven up an otherwise boring activity. Panty-free grocery shopping was a classic, and the light nipple clips had certainly made her nephew's high school graduation go by faster.

But rubber was different. It was a new sensation, a weird sensation, not something she'd have sought out on her own.

But Adam, it turned out, liked rubber. Liked it a lot.

His excitement had excited her.

And the way he'd looked at her once she wriggled her way into the strange garments—the way he'd gone down on his knees to lick at the cobalt blue rubber compressing her clit—made her get wetter and more open, despite not being one-hundred-percent convinced about the pleasures of hot, confining, unbreathing rubber. The dildo was helping with that.

She'd been trembling with excitement by the time they'd arrived at the Ransomes'; she'd gulped one glass of champagne and sipped her way through another in an effort to steady her nerves enough to act normal.

Admitting to herself that she had no idea what Laine was rattling on about, she looked around the crowded living room—a tribute to Martha Stewart and to Jessi Ransome's OCD—until she found Adam.

Her nipples felt like boulders, stretching the rubber bra. Her pussy jumped, contracting hard around the dildo, her lips squirming over the slick, wet rubber.

On the surface, Adam looked as standard-issue suburban as the rest of the guests, but she knew better.

Her slightly twisted beloved. Her demon lover in khakis and a dress shirt.

And right now, from the look of it, a demon lover in need of rescue. He'd been cornered by Gary Ransome for some work talk and it looked like Gary was still talking his ear off, twenty minutes later. He looked only slightly more interested than Cecily had been about Laine's budget rant.

He made eye contact with her, then gestured with his right hand—a little beckoning motion that was their prearranged signal for "Come here and save me."

Cecily touched Laine on the arm. "I'm sorry. I think Adam's looking for me."

"He sure keeps you on a short leash."

Cecily bit her tongue, sorely tempted to say something along the lines of "Not yet, but we've talked about trying it sometime." Instead, she composed herself as best she could over the insistent signals of her nipples and pussy and shook her empty champagne glass at Laine. "More importantly, I need to fix this little problem, and the bar is on the other side of the room."

"Next to Adam." Laine smiled. "You two are awfully cute, you know. Go on, lovebird."

Gingerly, very gingerly, she made her way through the party to Adam, each step a bit of sticky, wet, stretched, erotic torture.

He excused himself from Gary, slipped his arm around her, and cupped her bottom possessively.

Heat seared through silk and rubber, as if she'd take off her clothes later and find his handprint burned onto her cheek.

Adam kissed her on the nearer cheek and whispered in her ear, "How are you doing, my little rubbermaid?"

She winced at the bad pun, but had to confess the truth. Wanted to confess the truth, because it might get her home sooner, let Adam's cock replace the wonderfully tormenting dildo, let her finally reach the climax she'd been hovering near all evening. (She might have actually come by now if she hadn't had to use the bathroom, which had broken the cycle of arousal long enough to keep her on edge, rather than falling over the edge.) "Wet," she whispered back. "Sticky. Sweaty. A little sore. And horny as hell."

This time, Adam kissed her properly, a deep, loving kiss that probably suggested to everyone else that one of them was tipsy. She leaned into him, rubbing her hard, rubber-clad nipples surreptitiously against him, barely resisting the urge to grind her aching clit against his cock, there in front of everyone.

Gary spirited her champagne glass away. When they broke the kiss, he returned it, full again. "Glad to see you guys are enjoying yourselves," he said dryly.

"Oh, definitely," Adam answered. "This is one of the better parties we've been to lately."

Cecily mouthed, "Thank you," and sipped the crisp bubbly, grateful that Adam had answered. She was sure she couldn't say anything sensible.

"At last!" she exclaimed.

They locked the door behind them and melted into each other.

Adam's mouth ravaged hers. Adam's hands pounced on her sensitized skin. Adam's hands unzipped her dress, pushing it from her shoulders. It slid to the floor in a silken heap. She kicked it aside, letting her shoes follow it on its path across the hardwood floor.

Now she was wearing only rubber.

And seconds later, or so it seemed, Adam was wearing nothing at all.

Adam pinched her nipples through the constricting material, then bent to capture one in his mouth.

Strange, to feel the heat of his mouth, but not the moisture, to feel the motion and pressure of his tongue, but diffused. Leather transmuted sensation, too, but in a different way. For herself, she'd have been happier to get the bra out of the way, to experience Adam's touch directly on her skin and end the long tease.

But his expression, just before he'd buried his face in breasts and rubber, and the way his erection was butting against her, rock hard and, she swore, bigger than usual, gave her a thrill that made up for the subdued sensation.

He cupped his hand between her legs.

Cecily bucked against it, grinding into his palm, feeling the dildo inside her as something the size of a rocket.

He turned his attention to her other nipple and moved his hand slightly, circling her clit.

Slicked-up rubber slipped and caught, slipped and caught, tugging on her folds, making the dildo twitch slightly. Pushing her, pushing her toward the edge.

She rocked her hips, begging for more stimulation and getting it, feeling the dildo inside her, feeling Adam's arousal, feeling his hands and his mouth touching her through the rubber.

She fell over the edge, and would have fallen for real if Adam hadn't caught her. Her cunt contracted hard on the dildo, fluttering around it, and she couldn't tell if the next set of waves that passed over her was a second orgasm or the first one continuing. After the long buildup, the long tease, the release was enough to bring tears to her eyes.

Then they were on the floor, not caring that it was hard and uncomfortable, and Adam was peeling the panties off her. It was as if the orgasm had triggered some kind of time lapse because she wasn't sure how they actually got there.

Some of her skin seemed to come with the panties, after sweating so much, but she was at a point where a little pain was just one more stimulus.

The dildo slid out of her with a soft, wet pop, and its movement—and some evil things Adam did with his fingers while he was getting it out—pushed her to an aftershock.

Then Adam pulled her down on top of his cock, filling her with hot flesh where rubber had been. The rubber had been good, but this was amazing, and her clit, liberated at last, ground against his pubic bone, and Adam cupped her breasts, still imprisoned in rubber, in his big hands, and they moved together.

She rolled her hips, moved up and down on his hard length, listened to his groaning and to the small sound, almost clicking, that they made together because she was so drenched.

Cecily could feel another climax building.

"I can't last," Adam grunted. "Too much."

Might as well make it a real explosion, then. She grabbed the panties from the floor and used them to tease Adam's always sensitive nipples.

And as he gripped at her hips and bucked inside her, she touched herself and released that last climax.

"So," Adam whispered as they lay in each other's arms afterward—they'd staggered as far as the bed for comfort. "What do you think of rubber?"

Cecily thought hard before answering. "I'm not sure. I feel all clammy now, and it pinches sometimes, and I don't think it's ever going to be my favorite thing. But being at the party like that...wow!"

Adam nuzzled her hair. "Wow, indeed. I think we ought to send the Ransomes a note and a bottle of something tasty to thank them for such an exciting party."

SERGEANT PEPPER

Rakelle Valencia

'm a city girl. I have no need to venture from my so-called hovel and range forth into the land of "leather and lust," as my boyfriend fantasizes about doing. I like the city. I like my small apartment. I love all things compact and tight to the point of formfitting with no breathing room.

Dead cows pulled across my skin don't give me even close to the same feel as my black PVC mini–evening dress, with nothing between me and it but possibly a smidge of talc. And I highly doubt these dude ranch vacations offer the shopping I can find three blocks away when fetish fairs visit my fair city. Mmm... racks of rubber and latex and PVC...a dream for a bustling, hustling girl like me.

And no one says a thing at work when I arrive to sit in my cubicle wearing navy blue PVC slacks that stretch and cling, so shiny and elegant, from my waist, over my ass to my knees, then flair off of my skin to whisper and tease where they don't bind me snuggly.

I know my boss loves it. He rubs his hands together and scratches absently at his meaty palms when I walk by. I'll bet he's wondering what it would feel like to spank my encased ass or slide his hands over the smooth material that leaves nothing to the imagination or roll me in oil just so he could rub his body against me.

He licks his lips as he reads my slick-shaven lower ones through the tightly creased crotch. What he doesn't know, and cannot see, is how wet I get from walking the aisles of cubicles to the coffee machine or the water cooler. The wetness lubricates the PVC so that it slides tantalizingly through my slit and over the small nub that hardens quickly to become overly sensitive to any movement of my teasing garment.

On these days, I walk around as much as I can, then return quickly to my chair, yank a small vibrator from the desk drawer, and cover its sensual noises with the constant running of my printer, which is old and loud. I can barely hear the vibration after the pocket rocket sucks into my PVC-covered crease and sticks while I rock back and forth. It's in the effort to stifle the moaning, the squeaking of my wheeled desk chair, and the wanting to scream at each orgasm that my printer dutifully cranks out sheets of obsolete data, and my teeth chew into my lower lip.

My boyfriend actually wanted me to leave all of this for a week away on some dusty dude ranch. I did the horse thing as a kid. It's over. I left it behind. But if I humored him, at least there would be the nights at this dude ranch. I'd pack my newest outfit, which was totally outrageous, as was its expense. It'd be worth it. Just the thought of wearing it had made the suit worth it already.

My cell phone rang as I was sitting on my roller bag to zip it shut. I couldn't risk this suitcase under the plane. I needed to pack it lightly enough to fit in the overhead compartment. The ringing was insistent. I knew it was him. "Hello," I answered innocently enough, while trying to stop envisioning licking my own arms adorned with the lengths of long-sleeved encasements in bright colors of PVC.

He'd been sent to Chicago for a meeting. He swore he'd meet me at the ranch as soon as he was done and could get a flight.

Great. I contemplated not even going as I plucked the plane ticket from my dresser and opened it to read the time I needed to be at the airport. The brochure about the ranch was behind the ticket packet. I looked at it. The pictures of smiling family trail-riding parties and an entire side of beef roasting over a pit fire served to turn me off further.

The only saving grace about venturing forth to meet stink and grime was that I had bought city-chic jeans with the worn ass and knees already built in. To top those off, I'd also found a pair of faux-leather, tall, cowboy-boot-wannabes that would also look fabulous with the newest PVC purchase. Bolstering my spirits, I took a last look around the apartment, feeling as if I would never get back. I whispered, "See you soon." Grabbing my bag with one hand, I blew my bedroom a kiss with the other as I exited this life for a full week of another.

The short plane hop was terrible, as I was squashed against the window by a grandmother who used too much potent-smelling powder in hopes of covering up the stink of not showering in the last week. Extremely thankful to be exiting the plane, I almost threw myself at the cowboy carrying a sign for the dude ranch guests. That is, until I was overrun by a pack of screaming children clamoring to be the first under the sign in hopes that they could ride shotgun in the van.

He sent the families to the baggage claim after explaining where to meet up again. I stayed.

"Alone?" he asked.

I enjoyed how his eyes perused my body, dancing from my face to the floor and back again. "For the moment," I replied.

"Well, whoever left you to drift wasn't very smart. Here, I'll get your bag." His crooked smile was charming in a rugged, no-nonsense way. "The van is over here. Guess you're riding shotgun. I'm Vance, by the way." He held a tanned, weathered hand out, and when I took it, his grip was solid, confident and strong.

By the time we arrived, I swore I never wanted to hear any rendition of "Ninety-nine Bottles of Beer on the Wall" again in my lifetime. After parking, Vance went to get the key for my lodge suite, then walked me over. His butt looked so delicious swaying in those tight Wranglers that I quickly forgot the last hour's torment. Once inside, he said, "Here you go, ma'am," and swung my bag onto the foot of the queen-sized bed as if it weighed nothing. "You have a pleasant stay. And I hope to see you around the corral."

I tried to tip him and he laughed. "No, ma'am, I work for a living." I stepped up and kissed him instead. His blush ran about as fast as he did.

Dinner looked a little too rugged for my first night at the ranch. Luckily, I had packed crackers and cheese with a short bottle of sparkling wine. I unpacked, ate, and showered, then fingered this evening's outfit, which I'd laid across the bed. Dropping my towel, I flopped next to it, breathing in its new aroma and rubbing a long sleeve against my cheek.

Dave was due to arrive soon. The sun had set. Darkness filled the two rooms. In the distance, occasional lightning lit the sky, but it wasn't stray electricity that tingled my flesh, sending goose bumps racing along the lengths of my arms and legs. I couldn't wait much longer for Dave to arrive, and I certainly couldn't wait a second more to stretch jacket and pants over my bare body, feeling their perfect fit.

I dressed with sensual slowness, appreciating everything from smell to feel to finished look. I desperately wanted to lap my arms and rub a finger through the crease of my cunt to my ass. And there would have been more, so much more, as the suit heated and practically liquefied to me while my body moved around the room in front of the mirror. It was perfect. But I couldn't start now or there would be nothing left of me for Dave.

The wait was becoming unbearable. As the storm mounted outside, my sexual anticipation grew. I wanted Dave to look at me, stroke my PVC-encased body, lick it and bite it and torture the skin beneath. I wanted to see his white come splatter the shiny surface. And I wanted his waning prick to smear the spunk all over me. I could almost feel the sensations. My cunt grew wet, wetter than it had ever been. Twat lube had found a way to slip not only the length of my crease all the way to my ass, but also down the inside of my thighs.

I couldn't help it. I rolled onto the bed and rubbed on the overlarge pillows, humping and pumping in the slick warmth until I almost screamed with release. But I wouldn't. I couldn't. I had to and needed to. But I would wait.

My cell phone rang. I popped it open to immediately hear Dave's voice. "There's a storm that's holding the planes from flying. I might not make it there tonight."

There was a loud banging at my door in the same instant. "Folks who can help should get to the corrals. The cowboys are roping and haltering the horses to walk them off of the ridge. The rain's washing down the arroyo in a flash flood and we have very little time!"

That was that. Tossing the cell phone to the middle of the bed, I hauled on my black faux–cowboy boots and went out into the storm. My deep red suit with its PVC trim of gold braid caught a few eyes at first, but there was frightening work to be done with horses rearing and screaming as they were hustled from the ridge into the corral. The guests coupled with cowboys to get pairs down through the lightning and wash of rain. Vance was roping and haltering. He turned, just as I was there to take the scared horse from him. His look said it all.

As the last of the horses were pulled from the ridge with no tremendous incidents, guests and cowboys alike started filing from the corral to get under cover and most likely change from their soaked clothes.

The lightning had passed, but the rain continued to drive down. I felt each drop hit my suit with a cold exhilaration. Leaning against the corral rails, I didn't want to run for cover. This was a new twist to what PVC had offered me. I didn't care if I looked like a lost band member in a pasted-on suit.

"I'll bet you're not totally dry." Vance startled me. The wind tortured his yellow full-length slicker, ripping the sides open until I noticed that he was sopped with rain and sweat. His light-weight cotton checkered shirt was see-through, defining pectorals that only an outdoorsman could attain without looking like a gym bunny. His Wranglers were rain-darkened down the front but still advertised the visible bulge of his excitement.

He put his hands on the rails on either side of me. Twisting his head to the side so that his hat stayed on, he whispered in my ear, "I want to rub my cock all over that slippery wet ass crack of yours."

"And I thought you were a shy one."

"Lady, there's nothing shy about *Sergeant Pepper's Lonely Hearts Club Band*. And I am enjoying the show."

I lifted my breasts and stretched to follow one of the lines of PVC yellow-gold braid trim with my tongue. The rain splashed

my face and continued to create a thumping and stinging sensation along my suit.

Vance sucked at my lips for a kiss and gently entwined his
tongue with mine before spinning me around and placing my
hands two rungs down so that I was bent at the waist. His open
slicker slapped at me in the wind. He rubbed against my ass and
reached for a moment to follow the lines of my body, sliding
easily along the wet ensemble.

When he took his hands away, I heard his gritty zipper protest
at his yanking. His prick was fully engorged and the sodden
Wranglers were not releasing him willingly. His hard-on popped
out, slapping me in the backside.

I giggled.

"You liked that, did you?" He rose to his toes, riding my
crease.

The feel of him seemed bigger than I had ever experienced. I
reached back.

"Uh-uh," he said as he took hold of both my wrists to place
them in front of me and pulled my body into his, as his cock
followed the slit between my legs.

I gripped my thighs shut.

He hauled me slightly from him and slapped my ass. The
PVC mixed with the rain made a resounding crack that echoed
much worse than what my skin felt. But I had felt him. His full
hand on my buttocks was bound to have left a red mark.

The slashing rain washed between us, slithering down my
back. Vance used it as lube to hump and slide his dick first up
my ass crack then down between my legs. He still held my wrists
and tucked them into my belly as his free hand pinched and
pulled at my cunt lips before rubbing stiffly and quickly against
my blood-filled clit shaft.

I sucked the water rivulets off of my upper arm, lapping when it dried too much. I felt him poking and prodding me to ecstasy, but I wanted my fantasy. I wanted to see thick, rich cream spurt in ropes onto my red and gold PVC suit. I wanted my fingertips to play in his seed as if it were art I was creating.

He grunted. He bit my earlobe. His hands clenched and unclenched about my wrists until he let me loose to grab at himself. I took the opportunity to turn and kneel in front of him as he drained pulse after pulse of come onto the Sergeant Pepper PVC jacket. I looked up into his wild face and laughed. He heard what little the wind hadn't sucked from my throat. Then he watched as I swished his essence over my covered breasts and pricked at my nipples.

Vance leaned forward and rubbed his waning penis through the rain-mixed semen.

TIGHT SQUEEZE

Rachel Kramer Bussel

'm always looking for ways to show off my boy toy, Randy. He's fifteen years younger than I am and more than lives up to his name. Actually, he's my boyfriend, but that sounds way too formal. He doesn't mind *boy toy,* and I certainly enjoy the fruits of our lusty relationship, plus our age difference makes it even more fitting. While I've just turned the cusp of forty, he's smack in the middle of his twenties, both of us hitting our sexual peaks together. This means we're both eager to try new things, but he lets me take the lead since I'm older and more experienced. The age difference might give me cause to doubt his fidelity, if he didn't worship me so. I'm not sure if he knows it, but Randy has been the catalyst for bringing out my dominant side. Not just the occasional bad-boy-over-the-knee routine I've used in the past, but a kind of dominance that permeates our relationship. We're not 24/7 anything, but he does defer to me in all matters sexual, and has bravely and boldly allowed me to usher him into countless kinky scenes that he's enjoyed as much as I have. All he needed was a little prompting.

So the other day, as I gazed at his naked body, all rippled with muscles and sculpted to perfection, from his sleek chest with its perky pink nipples to his six-pack abs and flat stomach, down to the cock that just keeps on giving, I started to imagine what he'd look like in a catsuit. Usually, when you think of a catsuit, it's worn by a woman in my position, a woman in control, a woman who wears latex to shore up her sense of her own strength and dictate to everyone around her that she is the kind of cat that hisses, snarls, bites and claws. To show she's a feral wildcat who can dominate everyone around her with a single glance. But on the right body, I figured, a catsuit could be a sign of submission, a way to expose his naked, ripe body even more fully than if he'd been unclothed, to emphasize every luscious part. And the image of his nine-inch dick, just as perfect as the rest of him, nestled snugly inside a shimmering blue latex sheath, made me wet instantly. "Randy, come over here for a minute," I said, sitting back on the bed and parting my legs just enough to give him a glimpse of what lay between them.

"Yes, Marianne," he said, turning to give me a dazzling smile. As he turned, I watched his cock harden, and a vision came to my mind. He walked closer, and when he got near me, I simply ran my hands up and down his glorious chest, along his sculpted arms and over his pert ass. I felt him up, down, and around while he simply smiled at me serenely as his cock bulged, growing bigger and bigger.

"Just checking on you," I said before tweaking his nipples, twisting his twin nubs simultaneously as I watched him squirm and try not to flinch. Then I focused on pinching them as hard as I could, which never seemed quite hard enough to satisfy me— or him. "You have beautiful nipples," I said before leaning back and beckoning him to get on top of me and let me lick them while his hard cock rubbed against my skin. The one thing he lacks is a pair of heavy, beautiful breasts, the kind I could get lost in for days, the kind I love to be smothered by. Fortunately, we have a gorgeous minx of a girl named Eva who comes by once a week and lets me torture her breasts to my heart's delight. With my hands roaming along Randy's back while I bit and licked his nipples, I knew what I had to do.

When he seemed ready to explode, I sat up, leaned back against the pillows, spread my legs wide and ordered him to masturbate. "Come for me—and tell me your favorite color. Be specific." I already knew the answer was green, but I wanted to hear him describe it while he got off. As for me, I'd have been happy to dress him in any color, as long as the latex gleamed brightly, shined up so I could show him off.

The oddly juxtaposed tasks seemed to throw him off, but Randy knows how to get off in almost any situation. Pumping his thick, hard dick with slow, even strokes, he stared at my pussy but spoke to me. "Green, but a smoky kind of green, like a lush forest seen through a slight fog of smoke. Almost grayish green, but still alive, verdant. A green that's the equivalent of blood red, powerful, sacred, rich and demanding. Green like envy and money but pure, like love. Green like turquoise, green like visible camouflage. Green like the sun and the sea making love." I had never known him to be such a poet, and the power of his vision was making me wet. I relaxed my pose, and leaned forward, one hand between my legs, to suck him into those final moments of ecstasy.

"Green like coming," I said, not really sure what it meant, but like a synesthete, picturing the exact color as his cock entered my lips. I swallowed, taking his entire length down my throat, as my fingers dove into my hole, sliding in and out as I encouraged him to fill me with his come.

"Yeah," he breathed reverently, his voice gone as soft as his dick was hard. I looked up into his eyes, those malleable eyes that can appear any one of a number of colors, and saw Randy's green, the green I would paint him with. I came then, staring into his eyes, brown on green on ecstasy, as he spurted into my mouth and shut his eyes, taking his green gaze with him. In truth, they're more like a dusky hazel, but I know what I saw.

After breakfast, I took him with me on my errands, saving the best for last. He drove the familiar streets with ease, not asking any questions until we reached our final destination. It was a store that specialized in the kind of clingy, sensual, shiny fashions I needed. A high-end rubber and latex pleasure dome, where the staff specialized in handcrafted, body-clinging treasures. They'd made latex wedding gowns and see-through stripper outfits, couture costumes for celebrities and kinky hoods, harnesses, and bodysuits.

The staff all knew me but hadn't yet met Randy. We'd been so busy with our other adventures, I hadn't found the time to get him properly trussed up, but I was about to fix all that. I tugged him along behind me, and he shyly said hello when the bell clanged. His age was all the more apparent as he hovered back, deferring to me. "Well, who is this fine specimen of manhood?" asked the over-the-top, wickedly sexy, and very gay Jaime as he got up to kiss me on both cheeks before moving on to inspect Randy. I'd let him wear whatever he wanted, and he'd settled for an old Violent Femmes T-shirt and artfully ripped jeans. A fine look, but one at odds with the rest of the shop. I was wearing a black, low-cut sweater-dress, black Wolford tights with stitching up the sides, and killer black heels, ones I'd slipped into in the car; no need to torment my feet with these five-inchers unless I was in front of a crowd. Especially when I had someone else I wanted to torment.

"Hi, everyone," I said, smiling at the assembled crowd. "This is Randy. He's mine, so don't go getting any ideas." I never really knew what to call him—*boyfriend* was inadequate, *slave* also not quite right, *lover* too pretentious, and *boy toy* too diminishing for public use. But *mine,* was a sure thing, a truth neither of us could dispute. If I wanted to break up with him, I'd be in for a tough fight at that point. I'd cultivated the perfect level of devotion in him, one so strong he'd put up with my occasional excesses and adventures.

"We're here to get him suited up. Randy, take off your clothes." He looked at me, his eyes panic stricken, beseeching. He's what I'd call a reluctant exhibitionist; he can't plan for it or get into talking dirty about it, but once he's in front of a crowd, his inner ham comes out usually. I walked closer and cupped his ass through the jeans, rubbing my crotch against him to simulate fucking him. I whispered in his ear: "Baby, they need to get a good look at you to figure out just how the suit's going to fit you. I'm doing this for me, yes, but also for you. You're going to love seeing yourself—and touching yourself—in this outfit just as much as I do. Trust me. Have I ever steered you wrong?"

I knew he couldn't come up with a single example of me leading him astray, and I watched him keep his eyes down as his clothes came off. Even flaccid, his cock is beautiful, and I made sure to fondle it in front of everyone, once again emphasizing that it was mine. "Now go let Jaime take your measurements. I'll be right here," I told him. Sure, I could've watched, but I liked the idea of sending him off with strangers, making him squirm, naked, as they figured out just how to coat him in the green shiny slickness. Besides, I only wanted to see the end result, not the making of the sausage-like enclosure.

And off he went. I gossiped with the other clerks and tried to act nonchalant, but I actually was thrilled that Randy was submitting to this process. Sure, you could say he had no choice, but of course he always has a choice, and should he ever tire of my dominance, he is free to go. But knowing that he allows himself to enter situations where he may find himself uncomfortable, all for my pleasure, brings me such joy. I'm not quite the heartless bitch I may sometimes appear to him or others, and I know that pushing him beyond his boundaries is not only good for me, but for him. As we traded talk about people in the local fetish scene, time flew by, and soon my boy toy was emerging looking hotter than I'd ever seen him before. Amazingly, they'd had a suit in the perfect green made for a guy with just about Randy's build, who never came in to pick up his purchase, and on Randy it looked exquisite. Grand. Divine. All those superlatives and then some.

His body seemed to glow from the inside out, the extra-thin latex seeming to capture all the light in the room. I walked over and immediately ran my hands up and down his glorious body. I had to work hard to pretend that I wasn't the needy one in this relationship. He felt incredible, like some kind of sexy alien coated in a supernatural skin. I pinched one nipple, watching it pucker beneath the fabric.

"Turn over," I barked. I hadn't been prepared to see him suited up so soon. I'd thought we'd custom-order the suit, then have it ready to debut, but here he was, and the situation just demanded that I make good use of it, and him. "Bend over and wrap your hands around your ankles." The suit was so snug that his asscheeks looked truly obscene when he obeyed me, more so than if he'd been naked. Sure, we couldn't actually see his gaping asshole or hairy buttocks, but the fabric clinging to his curves left little to the imagination. I lifted my hand and gave him a firm swat.

"Ow, thank you, Mistress," he said, immediately correcting

his faux pas. I looked pointedly at the others in the room, glad
to see all eyes were on us. "Everyone's watching you, Randy,
so you better behave," I said, before delivering another sound
smack. I kept going, working up a rhythm, breathing heavily as
I went. Someone handed me a paddle and I immediately began
slapping his ass, hard. This was harsher than what we usually
leapt right into, and I knew from my former bottoming days
that being spanked with the aid of latex against one's skin only
made the rush that much stronger. When I chanced a look at his
face, I saw that Randy's cheeks were flaming red. He loved and
hated that all these people could see not only his entire body,
but how I treated it. If he'd thought the latex would somehow
protect him from their gazes, he soon saw he was wrong, and
the more I watched, the more I knew that this outfit would be
in constant rotation in his wardrobe. I spanked him until I got
tired of it.

"Stand up and face me," I said, looking down at his cock.
It was thick and hard, swelling against the latex, pushing it out
grotesquely. I toyed with the zipper going up the front of the
latex, the only thing marring its ultratight perfection. I pulled
it down very fast, and he flinched, rasping out something that
sounded like "Please."

"What?" I asked, letting the zipper drop midway down his
chest. Half-open, the suit did not have anywhere near the same
appeal, its symmetry broken, its glamour marred by his hairy
chest.

I pinched his cheek, hard, then cupped his hard cock through
the latex. "No, don't speak. I heard what sounded like a request,
when you should know better than that, especially in front of
my friends. You're going to wear this home, and keep it on as
long as I tell you to."

I could see that he wanted to say something, but I didn't let

him. I just told him it was time to go, to the grumblings of the
staff. It was a slow day and they had nothing better to do than
observe our little tiff. He had little to do but zip the suit back
up. He hadn't been polished yet, so I bought a bottle of polish
in addition to the suit and thanked Jaime for doing such a fine
job. "Anytime, my dear, anytime," he said, his voice dripping
with lust. I knew that anytime I wanted Randy to experience
some man-on-man action, I could send him to Jaime. But now I
wanted him all to myself.

I took what I called the scenic route, grateful for the nice
weather that allowed me to put the convertible top down. "Lovely
day, isn't it?" I said as we stopped at a red light. I reached over
and fondled his cock, and he shifted, torn between his desire
and embarrassment. "You look beautiful, do you know that?
Like a model," I said truthfully. He did, as incongruous as a man
in full-body dark green latex might look driving down a sunny
street in the middle of the day. Knowing that the fabric had to
be baking his skin caused me a special kind of pleasure. I like to
make him squirm, make him suffer, all in the name of cementing
my rule over him. Plus, he was pretty to look at, shiny and glistening, like an edible sculpture.

As I drove, I started to fantasize about other outfits, ones
just like this but with a hole for his cock, so he could fuck me
while he wore the outfit, or, even better, a hole at the back, so
I could fuck him. What I wound up doing to him that day was
much more mundane. I'd originally envisioned taking him to
some grand fetish ball and showing him off to all and sundry,
but the contrast between my rather basic goth all-black attire
and his glinting gorgeousness was too delicious. For my own
amusement, I made Randy vacuum the entire house, watching
as he lunged forward with the vacuum, then back. When he was
done, I saw he was covered in sweat. I brought him a glass of

water, which he drank immediately.

"So what do you think of your new outfit?" I asked. Of course it was a test; should he say he didn't like it, he'd be insulting my decision. But if he did like it, I'd want him to wear it all the time.

"I like how it makes me feel safe, like it's protecting me, and I like the way it looks, I guess," he said, not sounding so sure. I ran my hand along his belly, a body part I love—and love to torment. "But most of all I like how you look at me when I'm in this," he said, in a soft voice that made me melt. He was my toy, but I was his, just as much, and whether he knew it or not, he'd just touched the soft mushy center lurking not so far beneath my sneer. I pulled the zipper down slowly, grateful the removal process wouldn't take too long, because I couldn't wait for long. I kissed his chest, then took his nipples in my mouth. He moaned, and I tugged harder as I stroked his cock through the latex. When I was done with the first nipple, I moved on to the second, biting harder, getting off on the pressure. Then, that belly, that sweet sweet belly. I twisted the slight bit of skin there between my fingers, tugging and jerking it as I pumped his cock through the latex. I wasn't letting him out of his most expensive item of clothing that easily!

I wanted him to come, but in the suit, and when he realized I wasn't going to budge on that, he surrendered to my teeth and claws: my nails dragging over his nipples, my teeth dipping into his stomach flesh, my fingers tapping against his cock. I inhaled the smell of the latex, inhaled him. Then I had an idea. "Stay here," I ordered him, "and don't touch yourself."

I was gone for less than a minute, returning with a bottle of lube, one safe for use with his new outfit, which I was starting to see as a sex toy in and of itself. I poured some inside the suit, onto his cock beneath the latex, like some people do with condoms. I zipped him up to his belly button, then went back to jerking him off. He groaned as the latex slipped up and down his dick while I bit my lip and pressed my legs tightly together. Seeing me crouched down before him, an observer might have thought I was the submissive in this relationship, but we both knew differently. "May I?" he asked, ever so polite.

"Yes, Randy. You may come. You may shoot a huge, hot load into your new suit that I expect you to then clean and keep shiny and perfect. I hope you like it, because you're soon going to have a closet full of these, ones that bind you just as well as cuffs, that show off this cock of yours to perfection. I think we'll have to shave you next." The more I talked, the more frantic he got, and soon I felt him come inside his garment. It must have felt strange to him, yet wonderful, too. I let him take off the outfit, and his skin looked wet, slick with sweat.

"You made a mess—now clean it up," I said, ordering him to lick his own come off the smelly green latex. He flinched at first, though, as with almost everything we do, he really liked it. When he was done, I handed him the list of instructions for caring for the new suit to study, while I snuck off for a quick solo masturbation session, the smell of latex on my fingers and in my nose. Now I'm determined to tell all the Dommes I know that they should really think about this when they're dressing their subs. Next on my list for him is a black suit with a hood and sexy little ears, a real catsuit. I plan to paint whiskers and lipstick on him, but instead of snarling, he will purr for me as he crawls around. Oh, yes, the catsuit is ripe for reinvention, and I know just the boy for the job.

BUTTERFLY'S KISS

Thomas S. Roche

If you take a left off of Figueroa and then a right, right, left, down to the corner of a street without a name, and pull past the sign that says PARK-A-LOT, you'll see it: the entrance to the right side street leading to the wrong back alley. Pay the attendant, give him an extra twenty, and you might still have a stereo when you come back. If you're one of those cats with an AM radio, you just saved a Jackson, but go ahead and leave your doors open if you like your windows.

You're wearing something you shouldn't be, so I hope you've at least brought a raincoat or a cover-up, or things are going to get interesting before their time.

Down the side street, which I won't tell you the name of, you'll spot a few sleepers at the edge of the alley, maybe. There's a Dumpster at the far end stenciled with Bob the SubGenius, tagged with yellow Kanji, and drunkenly sprayed over it all is FUCK YOU YOU FUCKING FU, which is the point at which the boozer ran out of Dumpster and presumably lost interest.

Over the open doorway, red curtain shrouding the inside, there's a sign but no words, just a stylized spider, *Latrodectus hasselti* if you give a flying fuck, red hourglass on a black body. Under that there's a cat in a derby, always a derby, impeccable, his mug impassive underneath, eyes watching as you approach. His name is Regentine, or more commonly Reg, but don't call him that unless he introduces himself, which he's not going to unless you're Trent Reznor or the Marquis de Sade.

Walk up to Reg and say your name, either first and last or scene name. He'll give you a look like he just scraped you off his shoe. He'll fish in the pocket of his waistcoat, pull out a reporter's notebook.

He'll find your name, because you won't be there if you're not on the list.

He'll check your ID, maybe pat you down, take your double saw, jerk his thumb at the red curtain. At that point you'll either come to your senses and go home, watch made-for-Skinemax softcore and relax with your thoughts, or you'll hit the darkness like a lush hitting bottom. If you've gotten this far, like I did, you're going to hit bottom anyway, and the only question is if you're going to get up again. So walk, my friend, and let me tell you what happens, if you're me and this is last night, Walpurgisnacht, the day the music died.

When I last brushed by Reggie twenty shekels lighter, not sixteen hours and a thousand years ago, it was a dark warm night in April and my digital watch was striking twenty-three. I nervously unclasped it, stuffed it in my raincoat next to my camera phone—not allowed. The velvet brushed my face as I slipped through; it smelled of cigarettes and cheap perfume.

I walked through the alcove, shadow black but lit in over-wrought UV where the club cards were stacked and the Plexiglas showed the blue-white face of the girl who accepts the chit you received last time you attended, maybe looks at you funny for whatever reason like she did at me, then hands you a piece of paper to sign. You hand the waiver back with your Grant, or two Jacks and a Hammy, or whatever, and she picks out a stamp: spider or butterfly.

I stuffed my paw through the little hobbit hole and she spanked it with that wet stamp, hard, maybe harder than usual, fixing me through the glass with a supreme look of self-satisfaction. I drew back my fist and looked at it, glowing faintly phosphorescent in the UV: eight legs, big ass, and plenty of fang.

Next stop was the coat check—another wicked girl looking disgusted. I shrugged off my raincoat and she looked me up and down, her disgust fading to a neutral sort of acceptance. I was one of the crew, maybe, at least with my rubber hot pants and tank. She handed me a claim check and drew an ankh on it. I glanced back as I left; she was eyeing my knee-high boots with the lust of the fashion victim.

I brushed through a second curtain, this one black leather, heavy like one of those lead aprons you wear getting X-rays at the dentist. The scent beyond was the first that hit me, just like always, but each time it's a little different and each time it's intoxicating. If you've got a predator's sense of smell, which I often fancy I do, you can detect the night's cocktail just by drawing a deep breath. Tonight, people were drinking a lot of Johnny Walker Black Label and fucking a lot of ass. The beat from the twelve-foot speakers hit my breastbone like a hammer.

The crowd was tight, pushed up against the dance floor, watching selected bodies grinding together. People were dressed like I was, rubbered, or leathered, or PVCed, second skins in evidence on both genders but the balance running about seventy-five percent women, which is the finest gift Ulysses S. Grant could give me.

I squirmed my way through the crowd, spent twenty minutes waiting to order a Maker's from the tranny bartender, who pointedly ignored me a couple of times before finally begrudgingly serving me. I ordered two because I knew I'd want a second one and fuck this shit. She wanted to see two hand stamps. I ordered one neat, gave her a twenty, slammed it before she could bring me back my change, and told her to keep it and bring me another on the rocks. She did with a scowl. I backed my ass away from the bar and wriggled my way across the edge of the dance floor, looking for the spiral stairs.

The place was a warehouse, then a loft, then a club; the spiral stairs are a cheap industrial-looking sheet-metal hack job probably put in by the latest owner. They squeaked as I climbed them. I panted a little and sipped my drink at the midpoint, then climbed the rest of the way.

Top of the stairs, there's a girl named Kane with a derby like Reg's, but Kane's is paired with an immaculate white jumpsuit, a cane and one false eyelash pointed straight to hell.

I showed her my stamp; she frowned and shook her head. I read her expression: she knew me, knew the tarantula, didn't think we were a good match. Kane's a nice girl, despite, or because of, the whole loving-to-beat-people thing. She narrowed her eyes, told me, "Be careful, fucker," without saying a word, the slightest hint of crow's feet telling it to me since there's no way soft words could pass on the landing and Kane's way too dignified to shout.

I squeezed past her into the leather curtain and her nipples brushed mine. Then I was in past the leather and her hand was on my shoulder, briefly, and I was gone, into the black where the music sounds distant, blocked off by heavy insulation and the half-inch thick curtain.

High in the corners, some spacey New Age shit was playing, competing with the beat from outside. Forty, perhaps fifty people were crammed into the well-equipped space, eight or twelve gawky spectators, four couples crammed into corners going at it—male male, male female, female female, male female, I think—and half a dozen women relaxing and getting foot massages, back rubs, kisses on their rubber-clad behinds.

The rest were playing, if you can call it that. A female plugged and ring-gagged on a St. Andrew's drooled down her front while a six-foot tranny whipped her. A guy bent over on a sawhorse was getting fucked by a machine. A woman in a gas mask was bound and spread on top of a horizontal cage, getting a violet wand to her exposed genitals. There was a guy in the cage, fucking himself onto a bar-mounted dildo. And up on the low stage, where emo bands play at Chagrin on fourth Tuesdays, an impeccable female body was suctioned tight into a howling vacuum bed, every contour of her naked body bleeding through the latex, growing more visible with every drop of sweat.

The vac bed is a fun little device or a nasty slice of hell, depending on your perspective, which for me can change at any moment. A sturdy frame of PVC pipes, it's wrapped overall with an airtight envelope of heavy-duty latex. A victim—usually a submissive, for reasons I'll detail momentarily—crawls inside and the pipes, which are attached to a vacuum, suck the air out until the rubbery skin molds so close it all but crushes you. It feels like you're being buried alive. The slightest movement becomes an ordeal and is often impossible, depending on the strength of the suction.

While some vac beds are covered with black latex, or latex thick enough to hide the contours of the body within, this one was an almost perfect white, and thin enough to be seen through. The girl inside was slim and savage, spread and squealing, the sounds muffled as she fought against the crushing weight of the latex.

In a vac bed, you breathe through a tube, and this one was trying to squirm but unable to because the latex held her so tight, like a python digesting something still ever so slightly alive. The intricate outlines of her shaved pudenda were of infinite fascination to me, as were the gradually more visible outlines of the blue-black Sanskrit characters tattooed above her sex, growing discernible as a thin film of sweat made the white latex translucent, then gradually transparent. The former, the folds of her pussy, I did not at first recognize, but the Sanskrit's a dead giveaway. It was the labial piercings that threw me, or the lack thereof; she'd taken them out, I imagine, so as not to damage the latex. Three on each side, now nothing.

I dusted my second bourbon, sucked, cracked ice, chewed. The Domme operating the vac bed was six feet in heels, poured into a rugby-striped number short enough to show her latex panties and low enough to show that she didn't bother with the matching bra. Her boots left a trio of inches between their rubber tops and her dress. Her hair was cropped short, a bottle-blonde contrast to the electric blue stripe on her black dress. She held the wired remote, a simple attenuator dial on an ergonomic grip. She twisted the dial and the bed howled louder. I watched the girl on the bed fighting it, trapped, suctioned into the rubber. I remember that: the fighting. I remember it like it was yesterday.

She moaned through the breathing tube, almost drowning out the music and the sound of the vacuum. Then she humped her body against the pressure of the vac bed, not making much purchase, asking and not receiving.

"Another drink?" asked the girl in the pinstripe latex dress, and I said, "Knob Creek," and bent down and gave her the first bill out of my boot, a twenty. Then I was back to watching, as she moaned and fought. The Domme switched off the suction and left a huge gap of silence unfilled by New Age from above and Psytrance from outside. My ears rang.

The girl's body became slowly less visible as the tension in the rubber began to relax. The Domme gave her a moment, ran her latex-gloved hands all over the entombed victim's upper thighs, then into her, pressing as far as the rubber sheath would let her.

The woman moaned. The Domme slapped her. The latex glove came off and her fingernails came out, drawing great gentle circles around the captive's breasts; she shivered at the sensation. The nipples had little gaps of air around them. The Domme took care of that with a twist of the dial, and moans mingled with the howl of the bed as the latex envelope evacuated. Going full bore now, the machine crushed her again, and the victim writhed violently.

My bourbon came back with twelve dollars, which I left on the tray. I gulped, not quite feeling the two Maker's, thinking I should leave; there's death trapped in that Pandora's vac bed, and motherfuck if someone isn't about to let it out.

The crowd shied away from the captive's audible moans, muffled from the breathing tube but growing louder until they actually drowned out the scream of the machine. The spectators formed a half-circle that, contrary to the typical wisdom of crowds, gradually inched back as the action throughout the rest of the room slowed and stopped, as manacles came undone and whips ceased their movement, as foot massagers lost interest and turned to gawk at the screaming latex statue.

I edged closer. Slick in its latex cocoon, the girl's body now showed impeccably, every contour, every curve, every place I had put my tongue and my hand, every part of her I had tasted, every part of her I loved. Her name was Aiden and I should have fucking left ten minutes ago, but the third bourbon was gone and that wasn't going to happen.

The dial twisted down, up, down, up, down, making Aiden screech and seethe and pump her hips. I was now the only spectator within the Domme's space bubble, which is rude at any party—and at this one, it was asking for trouble.

"You," she said, pointing, without looking at me.

I stared, dumbly.

The Domme's eyes turned to me, and Christ, did she look pissed. I gestured, "Me?" and she stomped her foot.

The beat from outside the curtain went pounding into my breastbone, *bam-bam, bam-bam,* in unplanned syncopation to fucking Zamfir Master of the Pan Flute or Yanni or whatever it was pouring treacly out of the speakers. I think it was the *Blade Runner* soundtrack or some *Year of Living Dangerously* shit. I shook my head.

"I don't think I should," I told her.

She killed the vacuum; Aiden moaned behind her breathing tube as the air hissed back in. The Domme's eyes were steel. "Did I *ask*, Tarantula?"

I thought, be careful what you wish for, which is not a new thought for me and seems to be coming with increasing frequency nowadays.

I put my dead soldier on a passing tray, looked at the tarantula as if to tell myself it was really there. I climbed onto the stage.

From somewhere, the Domme produced a dildo with a flat base. She set it up and said, "Put it into her."

"Look," I said stupidly. "I sort of know this girl. It's my first night. I know her. It's my first night."

The Domme grasped my hand, planted the dildo in it, and used both her hands to force mine closed around the shaft of the dildo.

"I *said* put the dildo into her."

Without looking down, she unzipped the vac bed and sat down to light a cigarette under the NO SMOKING sign.

The crowd had surged closer, perhaps sensing that something especially dirty was about to happen. If only they knew. I looked down at Aiden, saw her eyes glassy and dull behind the frosted latex.

"Can she see through this thing?" I asked.

"Put the dildo in, Tarantula."

My hands were shaking as I pried up the edge of the vac bed. I forced my hand under, scenting Aiden's body, sweat and cunt pouring out to mingle with the sharp stink of latex. I tried to keep my flesh away from hers, but it was impossible in such close quarters; in a moment, my forearm was slick against hers, glassy as we rubbed together, like naked bodies fucking after an hour of slow, hard afternoon sex—

"Put it in her," snapped the Domme. "I haven't got all day."

I could feel the heat as my arm crossed her side, her belly, her hips, pressed in tight. I took longer than I should have wrestling the dildo between her perfect thighs. The dildo was not a small one. I nuzzled the head between her thighs, reached my other hand in, with some difficulty, to spread her lips. I could feel the tiny keloids where her piercings had been.

I hovered over her belly and read the Sanskrit upside down, for the thousandth time, and the first: *The butterfly counts not years but moments, and has time enough.*

I pushed the dildo into her; in the slack latex, she arched and squirmed. Her ass lifted high and she let out a moan. Ice and heat in alternating waves ran through me, making my rubber pants distended.

"Zip her," said the Domme.

I did, with some difficulty because I had never used this device, only seen it used. When Aiden was tightly sealed, I looked down at her eyes, frosty behind latex. Her eyes, what I could see of them, gave me no recognition. I listened to the sucking sound of her breathing. I was still staring when the Domme snapped her fingers in front of my face.

She had a spider on the back of her hand: a black widow, not a stamp, a tattoo. She was a lefty.

She took my hand and put the control box in it, forcing it closed. Then she held out a vibrator, a big rechargeable number with an angled shaft.

"Well?" she asked. "Make her come."

"I've been drinking," I said.

"Not enough," she told me.

"But I—I know her," I said nervously. "She's my ex-girl-friend."

"Then I'm sure you owe her a lot more than one orgasm. Start paying it back, Tarantula."

I turned and regarded her; I fancied for an instant that we made eye contact through that frosted sheen. Between her spread legs, the rubber was distended with the base of the dildo.

I hit the suction and the distension disappeared, as the evacuating envelope of rubber forced the dildo deep into her. This time, her wail drowned out not only the scream of the vacuum bed, but the fucking John Tesh on the stereo. She pushed up so hard against the latex sheath that even as the latex went taut, she bent her body at an angle, hips desperately hunting for the ceiling, until I turned it up high and the dildo disappeared all the way inside her, and she went slamming down against the padded table underneath and did not get up again.

Now that I was close, I could see more detail—I could see the butterfly on her left hand, too dark, too defined, too colorful to be a stamp.

The Domme was at my elbow, whispering with the scent of an Indonesian clove caressing its way into me. I wondered if Aiden could smell it.

"Twist the dial with a rhythm," she said. "The dildo will feel—"

I lost the last part of what she said, because I was leaning close, breathing hard, twisting the dial to see the perfect outline of Aiden's body go clear and defined to white and undefined, each time the dildo slipping out just enough that she wailed when it went back into her—not an inch, barely a centimeter, but enough. I watched the rhythm of her body, the trembling that came when she passed the first plateau, the violent shaking at the second, and then, I knew, it was just a matter of making it happen, and the moment was in my hand.

For an instant, I almost killed the vac bed, put down the vibe, flipped Domme Lady the bird and went home to watch Skinemax. I was a moment, a split second, from doing that, when I looked up and saw Aiden's eyes and something said she saw mine, through the frosted latex, through the haze of the machine's tight embrace. I flicked the switch and brought the vibe down, on high power, as high as it would go, just to hear Aiden scream.

She did, and thrashed, and fought so hard against the crush of the latex sleeve that I thought for an instant she was going to rip the thing open. She couldn't maintain it; she was strong, but not that strong. Her arched back went flat again as I pressed the vibe hard to her clit, switching it low, high, low, high, medium, low again, and then with the shuddering spasms of her naked body, high again, because her eyes were wide behind frosted rubber, staring up at me again, and whether it was me she was looking at or a hazy blur, I wanted it more than she did.

She came not by screaming or thrashing or fighting or shaking all over. She just went slack, stopped moving, froze there for an instant, and then a great violent jerk shook the table, and she was still. I gritted my teeth against it, because for an instant I thought I was going to cry.

I switched off the vibe, turned the suction dial to zero, reached out for the zipper.

"Did I tell you to free her?" came a voice from over my shoulder, velvet in clove smoke.

"Go to hell," I said, and reached for the zipper.

The Domme's hand grabbed mine before I could unzip Aiden. Our eyes met tight in the darkness and our breathing went heavy for a minute under the Enigma.

"Get out," she said, pulling my hand away. "Leave."

I dropped the vac bed control, threw down the vibrator, and stepped back. I looked at Aiden, heard her breathing regularly through the tube. I could see her eyes, but I was probably nothing but a blur, a white frost, a caricature.

The crowd was pressed in close, but they all cleared a path for me like I was fucking Moses.

It was five minutes waiting for my overcoat, five minutes to the car, five more minutes walking in a long perimeter around the parking lot breathing long and deep and freaky. Some guys on the corner puffing a spleef stepped out close in front of me and asked if I was having a good night. I mad-dogged 'em and they shuffled back into the shadows like a killer faced with a war criminal. I gave them the bird as I passed.

My car door was slim-jimmed, my glove rifled, ancient parking tickets scattered across the passenger's seat. There'd never been a radio to begin with. I started the car and leaned on the gas to warm her up. Deep in my overcoat I felt a buzzing. I pulled out the phone and just stared.

I stared through six rings, till it was gone, then again, another six, then nothing as the engine purred. I put away my phone. I put the car in gear and crawled across the lot, feeling it buzz again.

At the exit, I turned right, not left, and crept down an alley marked DO NOT ENTER.

She was there, crouched by the Dumpster, black raincoat a dark pool all around her feet. She stood under the Kanji and blocked out the YOU YOU, which with the way the shadows were falling made the Dumpster say FUCK FUCKING, which at long last kind of made sense.

Reg stood watch over her, smoking a long thin cigar and playing absentmindedly with a butterfly knife. He eyeballed me as I drove up on the sidewalk. I pulled up, leaned over, popped the passenger lock, pushed the door open. It creaked.

Aiden got in. I saw that she'd neither buttoned her raincoat nor bothered to put anything underneath. I could smell the rubber all over her, the stink of skunk mixed with the heady aroma of her sex, the familiar scent of her sweat mingling. You can always smell them, people you've been with; it's like a body memory, and I remembered the perfume of her in every cell.

She sat flat in the seat, breathing. In my pocket, my digital watch chimed midnight. Happy May Day, people.

"I like your tattoo," I answered.

She shrugged. "Yours?"

I held up my hand; between my sweat and hers and the pussy juice, I was sporting Monet's tarantula.

She leaned across, kissed me, her coat falling open. My fingers found the smooth lines of Sanskrit, traced them, pressed lower. By the time our lips parted, my fingers were wet.

"Drive," she said softly.

I stared at her a minute; her eyes were still frosted, but no longer by latex. I put the car in reverse. Reg raised his hat as I backed out of the alley, flipped a bitch, went right, left, left, and hit Figueroa going north.

CINEMA SHOW

Elizabeth Coldwell

When Robert told me he was taking me to see a foreign film at our local art-house cinema, I assumed it would be about sex. In French, probably, with lots of nudity and maybe a dash of kinky action to spice up the story line. He knows that's the only way I can be persuaded to sit and concentrate on something that comes with subtitles. Instead, it turned out to be two hours of inter-family squabbling in Iranian. Moving, well-acted and garnished with awards it might have been, but it was still my idea of torment. Torment made all the more exquisite by the fact I was wearing the anniversary present Robert had presented to me before we left the house—a pair of black rubber panties.

From the moment I slipped the panties up my legs and settled them in place, I had been acutely aware of the way they clung to the contours of my sex. Robert had shaved me as the prelude to giving me my present. It's a task he usually requires me to perform myself, but as if to emphasize that this was a special occasion, he had me lie back on the bed, a towel spread out beneath my bare bottom, while he gradually and oh-so-carefully sheared the stubble from my lips and mound. Now, I squirmed slightly in my seat as I wondered how many more times two very stubborn middle-aged brothers could refuse the opportunity to settle their differences before the film finally, blessedly, came to an end. And with each movement, it seemed as though every centimeter of the flesh that Robert had so lovingly denuded was being teased and caressed by the thin latex. My pussy felt hot, flooded with juices that were trapped by the tightly fitting rubber. I wanted to slide a finger under the material and touch myself, but Robert hadn't given me permission to do that and so I sat there, fidgeting and craving release.

Giving up on trying to follow the story line, my mind drifted to the first time Robert and I met, in a fetish clothing shop in Kensington. I had just moved down to London, a city where anything is possible and almost any sexual fantasy can be indulged, from a small northern town where you were considered a failure if you weren't married and pregnant by the age of twenty-one. I had been fascinated by rubber ever since I had seen one of my favorite singers wearing a shiny, formfitting black dress in the weekly pop music magazine I had on order from our corner newsagent. One day, I determined, I too would wear a dress like that, but even having tracked down the shop from which my heroine had bought hers, according to the interview that accompanied the picture, I must have walked past it about half a dozen times before finally plucking up the courage to step inside.

When I did, the smell of rubber assaulted my nostrils, stronger and more pungent than I could ever have imagined. It repulsed me, and yet it drew me in. I couldn't imagine ever getting used to it, but I had to have more. I was admiring a rack of rubber dresses, trying to imagine how the cold, shapeless and slightly clammy latex would look as it molded itself to my curves, when I heard a voice behind me.

"We've got a dressing room at the back, if you want to try it on." I turned to see a gray-haired man looking me up and down with a knowing smile.

"I wouldn't...I've never..." I stammered.

"Ah, a rubber virgin, eh? My favorite kind of person. Let me show you..."

And that was Robert, the shop's assistant owner, who took me in hand and made my rubber dreams a shiny, slippery reality. He taught me everything I needed to know about caring for my dress: how I needed to coat my body in talcum powder before pulling it on, how I could use silicone spray to buff the dull rubber to a stunning mirrored shine, and how, even if I had staggered in from a club at three in the morning, I had to wash the dress before I could go to bed, to make sure sweat and smoke didn't destroy it.

As rubber quickly became my demanding mistress, Robert became my strict master. If I knew very little about dressing for pleasure, I knew even less about domination and submission. Robert was my guide, my mentor, my silver fox. When my friends mocked me for being with a man who looked old enough to be my father, I just smiled, knowing that calling Robert "Daddy" could make him as hard as wearing rubber made me wet.

When I wore the rubber dress for him, I was never allowed to wear anything beneath it. He told me it was because the lumps and bumps of my underwear would show through and spoil the line of the garment, but I knew it was really because he got a thrill out of parading me around the scene clubs in nothing but a thin coating of rubber and a pair of outrageously high heels. I was always nervous about going out in public dressed like that; the dress finished a few inches below the cheeks of my bottom, and I was sure that if I sat carelessly or walked upstairs, I would be treating anyone who cared to look to a view of the pink, shaven lips of my sex. That, of course, was all part of the attraction to Robert, and he loved to whisper in my ear how he would buy a spreader bar and use it to secure my legs wide apart, so I had no choice but to display my pussy to the world. Though I protested, I was sure he knew that inwardly I thrilled to the idea of being forcibly, blatantly exposed. And when he embellished the fantasy, telling me he would invite passing slaves, male or female, to crouch before me and lick me out for his pleasure, I would have to bite my lip to stop myself from begging him to do it.

But what had always turned me on most was when he said he would find a way of making me wear rubber in a more respectable setting. Strutting around dressed to impress in a club where everyone was wearing some kind of fetishy costume was one thing, but sitting behind my desk in the office where I worked, with no one knowing I had rubber on beneath my neat little skirt suit, would be a new game altogether, and a deliciously spicy one. It would make it hard to concentrate on my work, I was sure, but for the thrill of spending a whole day with rubber next to my skin, feeling its sensual caress, it was worth risking the wrath of my boss.

So I shouldn't have been entirely surprised when Robert presented me with the indecently brief panties and told me I would be wearing them tonight. But now, with the film still showing no sign of finishing, and my pussy captive and wanting inside its black rubber prison, I was realizing the true price of indulging my fetish in public.

At that moment, Robert leaned over and casually draped an arm around me. The most innocent of gestures, but it enabled him to lightly touch my breast with his fingertip. My nipple stiffened in response, and as he carried on stroking me, I felt little twinges of desire flaring in my crotch. I wriggled in my rubber panties, feeling them rub against my sensitized skin, stimulating me beyond endurance. I stifled a whimper; there was no one sitting next to us, but I didn't want to alert anyone in the rows in front or behind to what was happening.

I knew that Robert was perfectly prepared to keep toying with me till the credits rolled, teasing me, and though he normally had no interest in the names of the location unit, camera crew or production assistants, he would be prepared to sit there and read every single one before he even thought about giving me the satisfaction I needed. I didn't think I could take much more; his stroking had become light pinches of my nipple, and I was squeezing my thighs together, desperate for relief. I knew it wouldn't take a great deal of this treatment for me to go over the edge, and I knew Robert wouldn't be happy if I did. But he had to be aware that I had been horny and wet ever since I had put the panties on, and that I had almost reached the point where the last of my self-control had evaporated and I would beg him to let me come.

Finally, I did just that. "Please, Robert," I whispered. "I have to come. Please let me come."

For a moment, I thought he would refuse my request and leave me frustrated. Then the corners of his mouth curved in a wicked smile. "Very well, but only if you do it to yourself and you do it here."

I swallowed hard. I had been wanting to feel Robert's thick cock inside me as I came, and I had been hoping he might drag me out to the toilets in the foyer for a quick fuck, my skirt up and my rubber panties down around my knees as he took me hard from behind. Playing with myself here, where I might be noticed, was more of a risk than I had expected to take. But

Robert was in charge, as he had been from the moment we left the house, and so I had no choice but to obey him. "Okay," I said in a small voice.

"Right, I want you to take your panties off and give them to me."

I glanced around briefly to make sure we hadn't attracted the attention of a nosy usherette, then quickly hooked my fingers in the waistband and hauled them down my legs with a slightly inelegant shuffling of my bottom. Somehow, it felt like a wrench to take them off; they seemed to have become part of me while I had been sitting there. Robert took them, still warm from my body, and clutched them as I began to touch myself. My cunt was hot and slick, as though it had been marinating in my juices within those panties, and I almost moaned aloud as I slipped two fingers up inside myself. In the half-light of the cinema, I didn't know exactly how much Robert could see of what I was doing, but I was sure he could hear the obscene squelching noises as I thrust those fingers in and out.

Growing increasingly oblivious to my surroundings, I sprawled my legs apart and sank down in my seat, strumming my clit.

"Tell me how it feels," Robert murmured.

"Good—it feels good," I told him, though I was finding it hard to form the words in my excitement.

"Do you like your new panties?" he asked.

"Love them," I said. "Love the way they feel, love the way they look." The pleasure was building in me, and I was breathing hard and rubbing my bare bottom against the plush fabric of the seat.

"How about the way they smell?" And as the first spasm of orgasm hit me, Robert thrust the crotch of the rubber panties under my nose. I couldn't help but take a breath rich with the powerful scent of latex and my own spicy cunt aroma, and I came like I'd never come before.

Robert said later that it was only a series of gunshots on the film soundtrack masking my squeal of pleasure that prevented anyone from realizing what I had been doing. Before the lights could come up, we snuck out of the cinema, me on slightly unsteady legs and Robert chuckling to himself and wondering aloud how my endurance would stand up to wearing those wonderful panties through an all-night Fellini retrospective the art house had planned for later in the year.

EXCHANGES

Stella Hunter-Smith

It would be a simple exchange, one garment for another. It would be quick, effortless, harmless even, and after all, Elise would be getting something in return.

Still, there were tingles in my belly as I stood in front of her closet. I looked over my shoulder like a bandit, expecting her to round the corner and foil my plans, though she wasn't due home for another hour.

I opened the closet door. What sat on display before me was dark and lifeless. And there were mounds of it, on hangers, on shelves, even piled in corners.

Stepping inside, I pushed aside jackets and pants, waded through thick, heavy material until I found exactly what I was looking for. It hung in the rear of her closet much like it hung from her body, plain and drab.

I grabbed at it quickly, snatching it down. I held it out in front of me.

How could anyone find this attractive, see it hanging in the store and consider it something to add to her wardrobe?

But Elise loved it. And, of course, she wasn't looking for attractiveness. She hadn't set out for sexy. This shirt, like everything else in Elise's life, had its purpose.

For one thing, it was practical, she had told me. It was good for protecting her pale, yellow arms from the sun when she was working in the yard. Many times I stood by the window watching this horrid shirt go floating by. I had seen it lying damp at the bottom of the hamper, had pulled it out of the dryer and hung it neatly in its place.

Yes, Elise would miss it for sure.

So, I took it. I stuffed it into a plastic bag and tossed it aside. From another bag, I pulled out its replacement.

And it was a fine replacement indeed.

I had seen the garment hanging in a window when I was on my way to lunch. It was enough to make me halt, cock my head, and ultimately go inside.

Elise would look good in it; there was no question. The stretchy latex would cling to her; the red would look wonderful with her golden skin and honey-brown hair. The halter would rest perfectly around her long neck.

It would be everything that godforsaken flannel shirt was not, and that was all I needed to know.

My task complete, I stepped back and folded my arms. I smiled, imagining the look on Elise's face. I closed her closet door and hid the bag with her discarded shirt in my own closet.

I went to the living room, where, sipping a glass of red wine, I waited for her.

If I knew nothing else, I knew that Elise was a simple girl. She was methodical. She appreciated routine and little disruption.

Me, I was a wild child, had lived on the edge all my life. It was what made us work, she had told me many times before, and this night, I intended to remind her.

She walked in at precisely twenty past five. Her baggy pants made a loud rubbing noise as she walked. A white T-shirt rested beneath her starched button-down shirt.

Her clothes swallowed her. Her shirt gave her the appearance of being flat-chested when in actuality what lay beneath were the most perfect breasts I had ever seen. What were hidden beneath those baggy pants were strong, beautiful legs that extended from wide, round hips. Stuffed inside those plain shoes were soft, pretty toes.

I kept wishing she would wear something that fit her, something that would show her glorious shape and curves, but along with everything else, Elise was a fan of comfort.

And comfort was the expression she wore on her face when she came to me and kissed me on the forehead.

"Why didn't you tell me the lawn looked so awful?"

That was my Elise.

It wouldn't have done to tell her that the lawn looked perfectly fine, so I simply said, "I guess I hadn't noticed."

She began unbuttoning her shirt. She stepped out of her shoes. "I'll hop to it, then, so I can get done by dinner."

I nodded.

I nodded and I smiled because Elise had disappeared into the bedroom. Her closet door creaked open. Hangers slid across the wooden bar.

I absentmindedly flipped the pages of a fashion magazine, throwing glances at the bedroom door, waiting.

Then she emerged. She took long bowlegged strides in jeans cut off just below the knee. She wore black work boots and long socks, and on her torso was a green flannel shirt unbuttoned with a tank top underneath.

Without missing a beat, Elise threw her straw hat on her head. She ruffled my hair and kissed me softly on the lips.

I forced a smile as I watched her walk toward the backyard.

I waited for the sound of the door slamming, the lawnmower cranking up.

I entered our bedroom and headed straight for her closet.

There, pushed aside, lost in a sea of baggy trousers and button-down shirts was the red latex halter.

I pulled it out and pressed it against my cheek. I breathed in its scent and hoped beyond hope that later, when Elise and I lay close, when she was touching me and I was touching her, I would imagine her in red, and I would be content.

I drummed my fingers on my lap. Impatiently, I listened to Elise kick off her shoes and drop her bag on the floor. She unzipped her pants and kicked them aside. Her shirt would be next.

She would want something comfortable to watch television in. She would look for stretchy pants and an oversized shirt. She would reach for her men's slippers.

Elise opened her closet door.

I waited and listened.

She cleared her throat.

I looked behind me at her leaning against the frame of the door. Her bare feet had made no noise and now she stood in white bra and panties, arms folded across her chest.

She had noticed—and why wouldn't she? All her clothes were gone, after all, and what remained in her closet was a variety of leather and latex, rubber and vinyl.

It was Elise's own fault, really. She had been constantly oblivious to subtle hints, so I had no other choice but to take a more direct approach.

And anyway, it wasn't like I was leaving her with no choice

at all. She could wear the blue leather corset or the long black dress. She could wear a mini or a pair of leather pants.

"Rona?"

She called my name softly and sweetly, interrupting my thoughts.

"Yes?"

"Babe, some things seem to be missing out of my closet."

I almost grinned, but instead I asked, "Are you sure?"

"Yes, I'm sure, honey."

I shrugged. "That's strange."

Elise cocked her head. "Well, what's even stranger is what seemed to find its way *into* my closet."

I turned toward her and pulled my legs up on the chair. "So, you gonna show me or what?"

And for the briefest moment I watched her, nearly trembling, afraid she would say no, afraid she would demand to know the hiding place of her flannel shirt and khaki pants.

But Elise winked and disappeared inside the bedroom, shutting the door behind her.

I watched the door, wondering which piece she would choose. I wondered how it would look, how it would feel against my body. I wondered how long it would take me to get the fucking thing off her.

Then it came, the beloved sound of zippers and the firm snap of elastic against skin.

Then silence.

Sick with anticipation, I called out to her.

"Elise, you okay in there?"

From the other side of the bedroom door came a heavy sigh.

"No," she said. "The thing is too damned tight."

But I wasn't about to let her give up that easily. "Well, let me see, maybe with some adjusting—"

The door opened and Elise walked out. "No." She held the long black latex dress in her hand, the one I had just picked out, the hot little number with the split clear up the thigh.

She handed it to me and placed her hand on her hip.

"They'll take it back, won't they?"

"I guess. But for now why don't you try something else? I bet you'd look dynamite in a pair of those leather pants. How about it?"

Elise shook her head. She looked almost disgusted.

"It was hard enough trying to get into that thing," she said. "How the hell does anyone breathe in that stuff, anyway?"

I folded my lips. "I don't think breathing is the point, Elise."

She shrugged. "Can I have my clothes back now?"

Just like that, without giving it another thought.

And I'd had it.

"Sure, Elise," I said, getting up from the chair. "You can have 'em all back. But first we'll have to make room in that closet of yours."

I ran into our bedroom and snatched open her closet door. I glared at the perfect row of garments I had spent months searching for, picking up and stashing.

It had all been for nothing. The thing may as well have been empty for all the good it had done me. So, with one sweep of my arm, I cleaned out Elise's closet.

I pushed pants, shorts and tops aside. I grabbed a fistful of thick, stretchy fabric and pulled. Hangers rattled. Garments fell to the floor. I threw what remained into a pile on the bed.

"There you go, Elise," I called out, "it's all gone. Your closet is wide open to be filled again with lounge pants and bathrobes."

I didn't care if I had hurt her feelings. I didn't care if I had gone too far.

I listened for her response.

The front door slammed.

At a quarter to one, Elise crawled into bed. She wrapped her arms around my waist. Her hands lay on my belly, her chin rested on my shoulder. Her bare skin was warm on my back.

She was naked.

And suddenly I was trying to remember the last time she came to bed with nothing on, the last time she didn't don an oversized T-shirt or pajamas.

Then Elise took my hand and guided it down between her legs and I realized she wasn't naked, she wasn't naked at all. As soon as I touched it, I knew what it was. I knew how it looked, what day I bought it. I knew exactly how it had looked on the curvy vanilla mannequin that stood in the store window, too.

I sat up on my elbow. "Elise?" I called her name into the darkness.

She kissed my shoulder and maneuvered me back down.

"You see, Rona, I was thinking," she said. "Maybe our original exchange wasn't fair. What do you say we renegotiate?"

Intrigued, I said, "I'm open."

"Good. Then all that stuff you tore out of my closet? You take those and I'll keep these, then we'll see what we can work out from there."

She rubbed my hand over her crotch. The black vinyl thong clung to her, lay against her cunt and hips. The vinyl was soft, so soft that if I hadn't known better, I might have thought it was her skin.

It was soft, and it covered her flesh in such a way that when I slid beneath the covers and bent my head down to rest against it, the swatch of fabric that covered her crotch was cool on my cheek. I turned my head slightly and inhaled her.

Shiny, black vinyl separated my lips from hers.

It was nearly enough just to lie there, to feel the thong on my skin and in my hands. It was nearly enough just to inhale it, until suddenly, it wasn't.

So overwhelming was the need to taste Elise, my lips trembled. I planted kisses on her belly and hips, tracing the edge of the garment with my tongue. I brushed my cheek against the thong, then lifted it with my teeth just enough that my tongue could slip beneath.

Then I kissed her there.

Elise tasted sweeter than ever before. She pushed with her hips, her cunt against my mouth. Her hands resting in my hair, she held me still.

She held me steady as the wave of her orgasm crashed against my lips.

Satisfied, I lay my head between her legs. I licked the taste of vinyl, the taste of Elise, from my lips, and closed my eyes.

RUBBER-PARTY VIRGIN

Jay Starre

S tanley was barely twenty-one. No virgin, but not all that
experienced, either, he had recently moved to the very gay
West End of Vancouver and was excited about it. Gay men
everywhere—on the streets, in the restaurants, the gyms, the
stores and the pubs and nightclubs. It was a dream come true
for a small-town prairie boy.

He had been raised on a ranch and had the lean muscles to
go with that vigorous outdoor lifestyle. He joined a gym right
away and began to work out regularly. He liked exercise, unlike
many who hated their time in the weight room. His best friend,
another young dude from a small town, was the one who'd
gotten him the invite to the party.

"Gary and Todd are really hot dudes. And they have the
best parties, I've heard. They asked me if you and I wanted
to come to their party on Friday night," Victor said in his
best dramatic whisper to Stanley as they dressed in the gym
changing room.

Stanley frowned. "Those two guys are old! Aren't they about forty?"

Victor rolled his eyes. "Yeah, one's thirty-nine, and the other is forty. But they're hot as hell, with more muscles than either of us."

Stanley had noticed them in the gym, always chatting to others who all seemed to know each other. Both were tall and extremely well built. It wasn't that they looked over the hill or anything, it was just that they were almost twenty years older than Stanley and he felt a little insecure about it. What would they think of him?

"They think you're a sweet piece of meat," Victor informed him, as if he'd read Stanley's mind.

"You're going, too? I won't be alone?"

"Alone? You fucking idiot! Probably twenty other guys will be there, at least."

Victor was the bold one, while Stanley was the curious but timid one. Victor was also full of shit sometimes, and Stanley seriously doubted if the two hot party boys had even noticed him in the gym, or called him "a sweet piece of meat." Neither had said two words to him.

Stanley arrived at the towering condo building with his heart thumping. He was shy around crowds of strangers, having grown up around more cattle than humans. Victor blabbed away at his side, excited and completely unaware of Stanley's nervous state.

"Oh, yeah, dude, did I tell you it's supposed to be a rubber party?"

The elevator door was sliding open and the hallway yawned in front of them, the doorway to this "rubber party" only a few yards away.

"What the fuck is a rubber party?" Stanley hissed to his buddy as Victor grabbed his arm and dragged him down the hall.

"Everyone dresses in rubber. Kinky, eh? Gary and Todd told me they'd provide some rubber outfits for us."

It was just like Victor to do this to him! Rubber? What was he talking about? Stanley had already been worried about how he had dressed, and now he was obviously going to be dressed completely inappropriately. How did one dress for a rubber party, anyway?

The noise of the party hit them like a pounding tidal wave. Piles of discarded shoes and clothing were heaped up inside the doorway. Men were visible wandering through the rooms beyond, and what they were wearing was like nothing Stanley had seen before down on the farm.

Gary, the redhead of the pair of hosts, appeared in front of them. "Glad you two made it," he shouted over the thumping disco music. He grabbed both their arms and pulled them into the closest doorway. "Everyone gets in costume here. What can we find that will suit you two?"

Gary was huge. Tall, and built like a barn, too, he seemed as big as the two younger men put together. He smiled and laughed and seemed nice enough, though, and Stanley felt a little better. But what was this rubber costume all about? What was he supposed to wear?

He found out. Gary held up a skimpy pair of what looked like shorts: banana yellow, glossy and tight. "Is that it? That's all I'm supposed to wear?" Stanley asked in disbelief.

"We want to see your sweet little body," Gary said with a leer and a wink.

He could have refused. But Victor was already tossing aside his own clothing, and Gary was dressed in a costume himself. Stanley wouldn't be the only one looking strange.

Stanley had been too overwhelmed to notice exactly what

Gary wore until then. A tank top and pants, all glossy midnight black. But as Stanley looked closer, he realized the tank top was not leather, nor were the pants. Were they rubber? The surface had a reflective sheen that seemed almost unreal. Gary smiled as Stanley looked him over and hesitated.

"It feels hot once you get it on. Take off your underwear too. Rubber feels great around your dick and nuts."

Stanley flushed and took a deep breath. Was he a chicken? What could it hurt? He wouldn't look like a fool when everyone else was dressed just as outlandishly. He was unaware that so far he'd seen only the tamest of the rubber outfits.

Victor was already donning his rubber. A similar tank top stretched over his slim but well-defined chest. This one was more of a navy blue, although it reflected the light so glossily it almost seemed black, too. A pair of rubber chaps fit snugly around his lean thighs but left his crotch exposed. He had a boner!

"You're going out there like that?" Stanley gasped.

"Sure. Maybe someone will suck it for me."

Victor's bold attitude shamed Stanley. The rubber shorts in his hands were skimpy, but at least he wouldn't be parading his stiff cock around for everyone to look at. Bright yellow, though? He would stand out like a sore thumb.

There was nothing to do but strip and put on the shorts. Gary watched with bright green eyes, red brows arching with interest as Stanley discarded T-shirt, then jeans, and finally his skivvies.

Victor slapped his naked ass playfully, which made Stanley jump and flush more brightly. To avoid displaying a rapidly rising hard-on, Stanley hastily stepped into the yellow rubber shorts. The material clung to his thighs as he pulled it up, stretching enough to permit him to pull it up to his waist but never losing its snug fit. He jammed his stiffening cock inside and snapped the fly shut. His boner rose to full mast inside the constricting material and tented it obscenely.

He felt warm all over. He actually felt naked, as if the rubber was his skin, and not clothing. It was very weird. Something else was weird, something he hadn't noticed in his dazed state.

He reached back and felt the clinging rubber that encased his ass. What was that? A slit ran right down the center. He felt it with his fingers. It opened up and exposed his ass crack! Fuck! He was wide open back there!

Gary was speaking. "What a sweet young bubble butt! Everyone is going to want a piece of that!"

A piece of his ass? Stanley was horny, especially now with the kinky rubber shorts on, but was he ready to give up his ass to a bunch of rubber freaks?

He blushed more brightly as his cock jerked inside his rubber shorts and leaked precome. The thought of all that rubber and getting fucked up the ass was more exciting than weird. Way more exciting! He vowed to keep an open mind. At least he would have an open ass, with that slit down the back of his shorts.

He took a deep breath and followed Victor and Gary out into the main room. As he walked, he felt the shorts open up behind him and he was sure his ass crack was clearly exposed. The rubber clung to his buttcheeks snugly and crammed them together, but still he felt like anyone could reach in and finger his ass, or his hole, if they wanted to. That image sent a shiver up and down his nearly naked body.

The scene he slipped into was bizarre. Glossy black dominated the room as men strolled around unabashedly, but there were other colors, too. Several splashes of ruby red stood out, some emerald green, and lots of dark blue. He didn't see any other yellow, though, and felt like he stood out a little too much.

Chaps, pants, rubber boots and tank tops were the most

common attire. But as Stanley mingled, he noticed other gear. Rubber jockstraps, and shorts somewhat like his, and even rubber gloves of black or green or red. A couple of dudes wore rubber masks that hid their features and transformed them into anonymous strangers.

"Look at that," Victor whispered to Stanley as he dug an elbow into his naked rib.

Stanley looked through an open doorway to another room, a bedroom. Two guys sprawled on a bed. They wore rubber from head to toe, one in black and the other in vibrant ruby red. Even stranger, they wore headgear that really seemed bizarre.

Like gas masks, the rubber hoods had flat nose nozzles and snaking tubes that curled out to connect to their mouths. Huge eye goggles emphasized their features and created a totally alien look. Stanley gasped as he stepped closer to the open doorway for a better look.

One of the men beckoned him onward with a wave of a rubber-gloved hand. Stanley's mouth gawked open, and he had no idea what to do. The pair watched him through goggled eyes. Whether they smiled or frowned was impossible to guess. What did they want?

"Go on, get kinky!" Victor hissed in his ear. His buddy shoved him forward and Stanley found himself stumbling beyond the doorway into the alien-inhabited bedroom.

Unable to see their expressions, it was their body language Stanley was forced to read. Both sprawled back on the bed on their elbows, their thighs spread wide. One waved him onward while the other dropped a hand to his crotch and lewdly massaged a bulge there.

Stanley realized the one in black wore an entire bodysuit that had a gleaming zipper up the front that bisected the rubber-encased man like a dividing line. The other in red wore a tank top that left a smooth upper chest exposed, and red chaps and a black jockstrap, all in clinging rubber.

Stanley approached, suddenly aware of how naked he was in comparison to this pair who seemed shrouded in their rubber flesh. Even their noses and mouths were encased in rubber!

He had no idea who these two dudes were in real life, but they were bizarrely exciting right there in front of him. He moved forward until he stood at the foot of the bed between the spread thighs of the ruby red rubber man.

A ruby rubber hand languidly motioned downward. The message was impossible to mistake. Stanley hesitated for just a moment, then dropped to his knees on the carpet. The crimson-gloved hand came out and clasped the back of his neck, drawing his face down into rubber crotch.

Stanley's chin, then his cheek pressed into glossy rubber. So smooth! Sticky but slippery, strange smelling but intoxicating at the same time. He felt his lips brush over the rubber, then he stuck out his tongue and licked.

He shivered, all at once aware of how far he'd come in less than twenty minutes. He'd been dressed normally at the elevator, unaware of what loomed ahead for him, and now he was on his knees licking a stranger's rubber crotch.

Stanley surrendered to the sensation. He licked the smooth rubber, sniffed it, and then licked up his own drool. The rubber hand on his neck was firm but did not direct him. It was his own nasty will that had him rubbing his face all over that rubber crotch, feeling hard cock pulse beneath the cherry-red rubber and then thrust up into his face.

Rubber hands began to stroke his naked arms and back. The dude next to them draped a leg over them and began to caress Stanley as he continued to mouth the ruby-red suit and shiver with anticipation between rubber-encased thighs.

He was aware of his ass crack open to the air. The yellow rubber of his own suit gaped apart as he knelt, and gaped farther apart as he spread his own knees willingly. He wanted to open up his ass. He hoped rubber fingers would reach into that opening and feel him!

His wish was granted. A rubber knee pressed along his naked thighs then up between them. Next thing he knew, a rubber-gloved hand slid down his back and over his ass. Rubber-enclosed fingers slipped into the crack in his shorts and pushed between the rounded buttcheeks.

Stanley moaned out loud, his tongue creating wet trails up and down the ruby-red rubber crotch. Rubber fingers plunged into his crack and probed deeply. Sweat broke out under the rubber shorts in a sudden oozing of heat. His balls and cock felt wet and slippery inside the clinging shorts. His ass felt open and slippery, and then violated as a rubber finger jabbed inside him.

Stanley bucked against the finger, moaning and tonguing with wild lust. He felt stabbed and speared, while the only thing he wanted more was to suck the cock under the rubber in his face.

The rubber man read his mind, or merely understood the frantic mouthing over his stiff meat. He unsnapped a rubber jockstrap and released his fat meat. The sudden smell and taste of real flesh was such a counter to that flawless smoothness of rubber, Stanley groaned out loud and wiggled his ass with total abandon around the finger probing it.

Stanley gawked at the rearing purple boner. The steamy flesh, veined and throbbing, of a disembodied and naked cock thrust out of rubber skin. He lunged with mouth open, drool on his lips, the taste of rubber drowned by the taste of cock. He slurped up the head and half the shaft as he realized now two rubber-encased fingers were worming their way up his tender asshole.

His naked thighs were surrounded by rubber thighs. The

man beneath him cradled his sides in his rubber chaps, while the stranger beside him sprawled over him with one rubber leg and knee rubbing all over his legs and butt. The rubber fingers on his neck encouraged him to bob up and down over that steamy cock, while now a trio of rubber fingers began to drill in and out of his palpitating anal cavity.

The two men made weird echoing grunts which sent shivers up and down Stanley's naked spine. His own lewd smacks and deep moans were more natural but just as nasty. He found himself riding those fingers up his ass and thrusting his rubber-encased crotch against one rubber thigh. He suckled on cock while he humped rubber thigh and fucked himself over rubber fingers.

It couldn't last. The bizarre scene was just too exciting. His cock fucked the rubber insides of his shorts, growing red-hot and slick from his own desire and sweat. The fingers up his ass made him wild, savagely probing his prostate and teasing his aching ass lips. His guts churned.

The cock in his mouth swelled and began to pulse. He pulled off just in time to receive a come-bath over his gaping mouth and snorting nostrils. The stench of come and the intense smell of sweat and rubber combined in a mind-blowing aphrodisiac.

Stanley's cock erupted. Goo creamed the insides of his rubber shorts, dripping down his erect shaft to pool over his balls, which were nestled snugly inside banana-yellow rubber.

The dude fingering his ass pulled out, but not before twisting those fingers around and probing really deep, which yawned open Stanley's asshole into an aching pit.

Stanley rose and stumbled away while the two unspeaking rubber men watched. The come in his shorts felt gooey and warm. His asshole felt hot and stretched and open. He was acutely aware of the slit in the back of his shorts.

The party noise was nearly deafening, and Stanley hoped Gary's neighbors were understanding. In a daze, he thought to look for Victor, but then decided he didn't really care if he found him or not. The sight of all those kinky outfits was now more exciting than ever.

Gary found him through the milling crowd, the big hulk encasing him in a burly arm and pulling him over to his partner, Todd. Just as tall as the redheaded Gary, Todd was dark-haired and powerfully built with heavy brows and an animal look about him. He grinned at Stanley before pressing him down to his knees on the floor in the midst of the swirling crowd.

"Guests get to suck off the hosts," he claimed with a nasty laugh.

Todd wore very little, the main item of dress a skimpy rubber pouch that bulged with potent manliness. He had a rubber collar around his beefy neck and a rubber wristband, all in gleaming dark emerald. He also wore a pair of high rubber boots that looked like they once belonged to a fireman.

One of those rubber boots kicked between Stanley's thighs on the floor and spread him wide open. "Ride that boot while you suck rubber cock," Todd snickered with an evil glint in his dark eyes.

Stanley was very turned on by the callous treatment, and rather than worrying about the jostling men all around, he reveled in the exhibitionist experience. He began to mouth and lick the rubber pouch, feeling thick cock and fat balls beneath. His tongue snaked out to lewdly slurp at the emerald rubber while he began to hump the rubber boot between his legs.

Gary was still beside them, and out of the corner of his eyes he saw the redhead take a bottle of lube from a passing stranger. Next thing Stanley knew, Gary was bent over his shoulder and running rubber-gloved hands down his naked back. Lube-coated gloves found the slit in his rubber shorts and worked goo all over his exposed crack. Those fingers slid deep and rubbed lube all over his sweaty ass valley. As Stanley slurped nastily over Todd's rubber pouch, that rubber hand worked more lube up into his aching asshole, a finger sliding in and out with smacking nastiness.

Guys flowed past, snickering, laughing, smacking Stanley's exposed ass or ruffling his golden-blond hair. He sucked the rubber pouch with real fervor, loving the taste of the slick rubber and the feel of the potent male underneath. His hands had come up and greedily groped Todd's naked butt. Rubber straps from the pouch encased and surrounded the muscular globes, but left the crack open for Stanley's feverish exploration.

While he humped rubber boot and got felt up by Gary's lubed glove, he worked his own hands deep into Todd's powerful butt valley. Todd stared down at him with dark eyes and nodded. Stanley nuzzled the rubber pouch with a gasp and crammed his fingers up a steamy asshole.

Todd began to hump Stanley's face, his cock beneath the pouch a throbbing rod of iron. The fingers up Todd's ass were enough to drive him to orgasm. He held Stanley's face against his pouch and began to jerk and twitch from head to toe.

Stanley felt supremely satiated, not that he had orgasmed again, but that he had gotten this stud off with his kneeling subservience. He rubbed his naked crack over the rubber boots briefly before standing back up on wobbly legs. He was immediately pulled off into the crowd by another hand on his arm.

It was a vortex of rubber hands fondling his ass, rubber crotches opening up to release steamy cocks, and strangely attired men who seemed intent on nothing less than an orgy of rubber sex.

Stanley eventually ran into Victor, both of them addled from numerous sexual encounters and the release of inhibitions that had them looking at each other like strangers. They blinked and laughed and embraced, then wandered off to see what other new discoveries they could make.

Stanley found himself back in the bedroom with the two rubber freaks in their bizarre gas masks. They waved him forward again, and he ended up where he had started. This time the one with the zipper down the front of his rubber suit opened it up and revealed a chiseled torso and throbbing boner. Stanley cradled against him, sliding his hands inside the rubber suit on slippery, sweaty flesh. The other in red mounted Stanley from behind and fucked his lubed ass through the slit in his rubber shorts.

Slithering over and under rubber, Stanley moaned out his second orgasm with spewing cock up the ass and spewing cock in his hand. He had only room for one thought in his dazed mind.

How would he ever go back to who he once was? Stanley the farm boy was now Stanley the rubber freak.

And he liked it.

THE BALLOONATICS

Gregory L. Norris

*H*elmut," she said.

His dick tingled in response to the musical sound of her voice. She didn't address him as Hel-*moot,* insinuating that he was invisible, or Hel-*mutt,* as though he were a low-breed dog, but close enough to Hel-*met* to believe she was talking to the head of his cock as much to the one above his crisp black bow tie.

"Or should I call you 'Agent Verland?'"

"No need for formality, Agent Pommers. Besides, I prefer the former."

So did Helmut's dick, which swelled in response to the clearing of her throat. Cold tingles teased his flesh along that sensitive patch of skin between his balls and his asshole, so like that feeling of sitting naked on a balloon, crushing it beneath your buttcheeks, the explosion of its surrender gusting over your most private areas, a stray tentacle or two of its plundered corpse snapping against you—hard—in one final act of defiance. Her voice was that powerful; Helmut realized he'd gotten painfully erect.

"In that case, please call me Vanessa."

Helmut shifted his pale blue eyes to his right, and the bar seat Vanessa Pommers now occupied. A second glance confirmed his first impression: she was the hottest piece of tail he'd ever crossed paths with. Black hair in a bob, just this side of short enough to be androgynous, eyes as eerily green as his were blue, full red lips, long shapely legs in black stockings, the rest hidden by an ostentatious full-length coat of shiny red material. She looked like the shapeliest animal ever twisted into existence by the hands of a party-game magician. He wanted to sit on her, see if she would pop beneath his asshole, tickle his balls. Those, in response, felt heavy and loose, so full of come and desire, he imagined them sliding down his pants, all the way to his ankles, one apiece.

He swiveled his hips, pinning his stiffness at an awkward angle along his left leg, and extended a hand.

"Vanessa Pommers," Helmut sighed. He released her from the shake and raised a pointer to beckon the bartender.

The slow curling motion of his finger elicited a purr. "I love how you say my name." She ordered a dry martini. Pure class. "It sounds so...*dirty,* as though you're talking to certain...parts of me, Helmut. *Helmut,*" she repeated. "Your name is so powerful, so phallic."

"Vanessa Pommers," Helmut said, licking his lips around the words.

Her drink arrived. Vanessa sipped it, while Helmut mentally undressed her.

"Nice coat."

"This little number? It's all a part of the disguise, the mission."

"You don't look undercover."

"You haven't seen under the covers. Yet."

Coyly, Vanessa unbuckled the coat and let the two halves fall open. Helmut saw she would have been naked underneath, if not for the matching rubber bra and panties, spray-painted onto a landscape of pale flesh.

"For our needs, I'm covered, Agent Verland." Vanessa ran her tongue around her red, red lips. "I mean, *Helmut.*"

"If you keep saying my name like that, you magnificent bitch, you'll be covered with my seed."

Vanessa closed her coat, sipped her drink, smiled that luscious red smile. Helmut ached.

"Working with you," she said, "is exhilarating, like that sting you feel when a rubber band shot in your direction strikes naked thigh."

Helmut adjusted his straining erection. He wasn't surprised to discover it was leaking a stain of wetness into the tent above his crotch. "I'd love to launch a hundred your way."

"Once," she continued. "I wrapped a dozen around a fellow agent's johnson. Skinny tan ones. A few thick colored bands, blue and purple, the kind they use to bunch root vegetables together with. How ironic is that? Right around his balls, too. Before long, he was blue and purple and begging for release."

"Marry me," Helmut said.

Vanessa pursed her lips. "First, we have to infiltrate, then confiscate. As you know, there exists a secret society with plans to overthrow the status quo. All thanks to their new wrinkle in science."

"So the plan is to infiltrate, confiscate, dominate, devastate... and then copulate?"

"Perhaps we should move that last part forward in the queue," Vanessa said, tipping her eyes toward the obvious bulge in Helmut's tuxedo pants. "Unless, of course, you'd prefer to masturbate."

The men's room attendant, an older Latino with a cheery smile, wiped the counter down and removed his seat to guard the door from the outside, a hundred-dollar tip richer.

Vanessa opened her coat and hopped onto the counter. The squeak of her rubber-covered ass gliding across the granite counter was magical, melodious. She crossed her legs, but Helmut soon uncrossed them. Lowering between her knees, he stole a look at his reflection in the mirror: short blond hair in an athletic brush cut, ghostly blue gaze, and rugged good looks that belonged to a modern-day specimen of man, stylishly decked out in full black tie and jacket. But for an instant, he found himself staring into the face of a primitive savage, a creature that worshipped fire, feared the night, and lived in a cave. Her wiles had devolved him.

Helmut yanked the rubber panties halfway off Vanessa's ass, felt them resist, and released them. They snapped backward, ricocheting against bare flesh. Vanessa bit back a howl. A wicked smile blossomed on her lips.

"You naughty, naughty girl…"

There was enough give to work them aside, to expose her pretty pink slit without removing them completely—which suited both participants just fine.

"The company worries that the enemy agents are planning an aerial assault," she said between sips for breath.

"Using blimps," Helmut said.

Teasing her clit with his thumb, he spread her lips, finding her not only wet, but flowing. He fucked her, in and out, using a long, lone finger. Helmut's mouth feasted. Vanessa's sopping pussy tasted sweet, with just a hint of rubber. Heavenly.

"Yes, blimps, *balloons*. You've been fully briefed."

"Debriefed," Helmut corrected, injecting his tongue into her.

Vanessa groaned a symphony of indecipherable, half-formed words in response.

Helmut stood. That his cock didn't punch through his pants and throw itself upon her surprised him. "Several transactions between the go-between, Dinsmore Corp., and a major airship manufacturer…"

Vanessa slid off the counter and down to her knees. Unzipping his pants, freeing his length and balls, she said, "The application is new, lightweight, quite explosive if you consider the ramifications. The company obtained a sample during a night raid on a suspected laboratory last month. They found it to be extremely effective, volatile in terms of what it could do…."

Her words gusted across Helmut's cock, now released to thrust up into the curvature that signaled its greatest stiffness. His erection had gone from merely pink to the marbled red-purple color of meat-counter selections. Helmut's foreskin had become a noose; his balls drooped halfway to the floor. The neat landing strip of trimmed blond hair above his root made all of it look even bigger.

"Your cock is wetter than my pussy," she said. "I want to chew on it, like it's one gigantic pencil eraser."

The gentle scrape of her teeth, the liquid warmth of Vanessa's tongue gliding down his shaft, tickling his balls—these little slices of paradise occurring in the men's room of the city's most exclusive private watering hole—were almost secondary to the sound of slick pussy being rubbed against even slicker rubber panties.

Vanessa sucked each bloated, hairless ball, one at a time. She pushed Helmut's pants to his knees and wormed a finger into his asshole. Her nine other talons gently raked his muscled cheeks.

"I'm thirty-two, not eighteen," Helmut sighed, "but if you keep doing that, I'm going to be forced to fuck that glorious cunt of yours with my tongue, not my tool."

Vanessa rose, a wicked little smirk curling on her lips. She reached into one of the coat's pockets and fished out a foil packet.

"We can't have you ejaculating prematurely, not with the fate of company and country in jeopardy."

Helmut tipped his chin at the rubber. "Company issue?"

"Of course."

Helmut reached for it.

Vanessa drew back, putting it out of reach. "Allow me."

She tore open the foil. Mercifully, Helmut saw, the condom was extra large. But instead of rolling it down the slope of his length, Vanessa shook it out into a tube and blew into it, making a cock-shaped beige balloon. She then deflated the balloon, formed a knot around Helmut's shaft and balls, and tied it tightly. The insane pressure sent Helmut to the tops of his toes in his sharp black loafers.

"A little trick I picked up from another agent. You've heard about 'the Anselmo Incident?'"

"Let me show you one I picked up from an enemy agent who could insert five rubber balls into her..."

"Wait, I'm not done yet," Vanessa interrupted.

She pulled another rubber out of her coat pocket, tore the packet open, and popped the collapsed latex ring into her mouth. Lowering to her knees once more, she took his straining length back into her mouth. Every inch of Helmut's flesh erupted with pins and needles as he realized what she was doing.

Agonizing seconds later, she removed her mouth from his cock. Helmut glanced down to see the condom wrapped perfectly around his manhood, rolled into place without the aid of a single finger.

He grabbed Vanessa by the hair and bent her over the counter. There, he rough-fucked her to the most intense climax in recent memory, one so powerful, he nearly forgot about the dangerous mission that had brought them together for the night.

Helmut eased his cock between Vanessa's tits.

"Shall I remove this first?" she said, indicating the red rubber bra.

He grunted a negative. With her on her knees before him, his reawakened length gliding freely through her cleavage, he found himself again facing the savage in the mirror.

"Wait," he grunted. "Wait..."

Helmut's cock drooled across Vanessa's red rubber tits. The drag of his balls along her torso was almost too much to process. Oh, and when she tugged on them...

"Now!"

Vanessa maneuvered her fingers behind his scrotum. She gave the condom tied in a figure eight around his cock and balls a final tug before releasing it. The room dissolved around Helmut. He moaned. His second orgasm of the early night nailed her, right in those gorgeous green eyes.

"I loved that bit at the end. You're a hell of a marksman," she said some minutes later, as they cleaned up.

Helmut picked one of the empty, dead rubbers from among the many discarded in the sink and snapped it against the taut pink nipple that had somehow gotten dislodged from her bra during the final thrusts of his tit-fuckery. Vanessa yelped.

"Stop that, please," she begged. "If you don't, I'm going to want you to fuck me for a fourth time, which means we're going to be late to the party, and time is of the essence..."

She applied a final touch of lipstick. "You know the two seditionists we will be looking for. The woman, Lady Darbi Dinsmore, she could be sympathetic to the cause, as we believe she doesn't fully realize where her late husband's millions are being channeled. The man she's with, Victor Rubel, has been identified as our prime target. He's mean and tall, ex-military. This is all a big game to Darbi, who fancies herself an entrepreneur now that her industrialist husband is out of the picture. But Rubel...this is his raison d'être. He's an outcast, the type of man who has always resented authority and the status quo."

Helmut grabbed his crotch and shook it. "I've seen the prick's dossier. The company knows quite a bit about his plans for the new world order."

"The nightcrawler who tailed him—and led to our raid on his laboratory—learned he and Lady Darbi Dinsmore will be attending this private gathering upstairs."

"What if they won't let us in?"

Vanessa gave her panties a snap, then buttoned up her coat. "We're covered, Agent Verland."

She sucked in her freshly painted lips, exhaled a cool sigh into his face, upon which a trace of his musk could be detected.

"Helmut. I'd say crashing that party is the least of our worries. Are you packing, just in case?"

"You already know what I'm packing, Agent Pommers. Agent Vanessa Pommers."

She crushed her lips to his and ogled the meaty fullness of his still-hard dick, a silent promise of the fun that would follow the danger waiting for them several floors up.

A pair of hulking gorillas in pinstriped tuxedos guarded the doors to the Rubber Room.

"You here for the party?" one ape asked, a soupçon of New York accent in his voice.

Tethered to Helmut's arm, Vanessa slinked toward the door. "What do you think, big boy?"

The gorilla on the right grunted and opened the door, waving them through.

Sultry music slithered out, the kind you hear during runway fashion shows. With it came a mélange of scents: rubber and plastics, aftershave, sweat, and pussy, all blended together, too bewitching to resist. Helmut entered first.

Topless serving women dressed in rubber thongs and high heels swept the room, their trays covered with champagne flutes. An equal number of ripped, athletic surfer types wearing rubber jockstraps and high-top sneakers offered similar lubrication to the crowd.

There were no tables or chairs in the vast room, only a multitude of beds covered in rubber sheets. Upon these beds writhed dozens of glistening body parts: a length of creamy white thigh pinned beneath a man's hairy ass and a pair of loose, bouncing balls that rivaled Helmut's own in fullness, a bare foot with toenails painted black being worshipped by a goatee, a fourway in which two well-dressed men were grinding hips together, mouths cautiously touching, hands groping. The pair of women Helmut assumed had come with the equation had hitched up their couture skirts—great mats of sequin-beaded rubber—and were grinding their pussies together, heads tossed back, faces screwed up in expressions of ecstasy.

"Agent Verland," Vanessa said, her voice sharp as the whipcrack of an exploding balloon.

Helmut faced her. "Yes?"

"Focus. We're not here for *them*."

"Jealous?" Helmut teased. Her lack of an answer was answer enough. "Would you consider engaging in a little of that kind of girl-on-girl action for me once we've obtained our mission objective?"

"Of course," Vanessa said. "So long as you engage in a little of that kind of action for me first."

She tipped her chin toward the two well-dressed men. One's mouth was now wrapped around the other's cock, which hung openly from unzipped tuxedo pants.

"Only if the mission depends upon it," Helmut grumbled.

But Vanessa was correct—he needed to focus. Helmut scanned the rest of the room, then the ceiling. That was when he saw them, the hundreds, perhaps thousands, of balloons. Reds and whites and fleshy pinks, suspended overhead behind a thin screen of mesh. Helmut's cock, which hadn't stayed soft in his pants all night, swelled back to its fullest hardness.

"Magnificent," he growled.

"Helmut," Vanessa whispered, her voice sweet, musical, a siren's song speaking more to his dick than his ears.

Helmut blinked and dragged his eyes down from the ceiling. "What?"

"There...it's them!"

Helmut followed Vanessa's prompt, into the crowd of bodies.

There they were.

The enemy.

Rubel—the cur, the scalawag, the seditionist—strutted toward one of the female drink servers, Lady Darbi Dinsmore hanging on his arm. *Rubel,* with his close-cropped black hair and a jagged lightning bolt of a scar slicing down one cheek, looking so ridiculously trendy in his tuxedo and flip-flops, his enormous, hairy bare feet exposed for all to see. As he passed by the serving wench, the brutishly attractive enemy of the company tweaked her nipple.

Helmut drew in a deep breath, held it, and then just as deeply launched it through his nostrils, like an angry bull readying to charge. He wanted to take Rubel down, crush him, even if it meant having to fuck him in order to do it. Images of the company's raid on Rubel's secret laboratory filtered through his rage: the sheets of clean plastic guarding the entrance to the lab, the workers dressed in white, poring over their new application, the shouts of angry voices, the defiance...the raw, big balls of it all!

Steeling himself, Helmut curled his muscled arm around Vanessa's. "Come on. You work on Lady Darbi. Get her to cut off her funding. I'll handle Rubel."

"Agreed."

The distance—twenty or so meters around an outcrop of beds and naked flesh—felt more like a gulf of kilometers. By the time they reached the couple, Lady Darbi was on her knees, performing a lewd act that wasn't very ladylike. Rubel had a hand on the back of the jeweled chignon clip holding her hair in place. His gold thumb ring glittered among the woman's locks.

A thumb ring! Helmut thought, snorting his displeasure out loud. Around that big hairy digit, it looked more like the cock ring of a madman. Ill-gotten gains had bought Ruble that band, and Helmut planned to knock it from his knuckles.

"Victor Rubel," he bellowed.

Rubel's eyes, half-closed as he savored the lady's suckling lips, snapped open like shades drawn too tightly. "How dare you use my real name here! This is supposed to be an anonymous gathering."

"The entire world will know what a dangerous scoundrel you are, Rubel—unless you stop your activities at once."

"Dangerous activities?" Rubel huffed. "Only to you. Which company do you work for? Condomaximum? Pleasure-gasm? Skintimate?"

"Who we represent is none of your concern." Vanessa grabbed Lady Darbi by the collar of her rubber dress and hauled her to her feet. Her lips and Rubel's hairy, veiny cock made a loud popping sound as they were forcibly separated.

"Get your hands off me," Lady Darbi protested, shaking free of Vanessa's grip. She folded her arms, licked her glistening lips.

Helmut cast a glance at Rubel's gnarled pole of a dick, saw that it was wet with a mix of saliva and precome, and delighted in the knowledge they'd interrupted his celebration.

"Lady Darbi, this man whose enterprise you've been funding," Helmut said, waving a hand at Rubel. "This man whose hairy root vegetable you've been snacking upon, is poised to disrupt the global economy!"

"You mean, disrupt your profit margin," Rubel snorted, "with a new high-end condom, ultralight, superprotective, but as thin and unobtrusive as a layer of skin! And with the Dinsmore millions to back me up, we're going to make billions!"

A smug smile on her wet lips, Lady Darbi moved to support her partner for the evening. Vanessa grabbed her, putting her in an armlock. Lady Darbi yelped.

"It will never happen, Rubel," Vanessa hissed.

"That's what you think," Rubel fired back. And then he shook his drooling grotesquery of a cock. "You, and you—all of you can suck my dick!"

That did it. In a flash, Helmut was upon him. They toppled over, struck a mattress, bounced, and were hurled onto the floor between beds. Somebody screamed.

During the scrum, Helmut caught a bit of dialogue from the next bed over.

"Oh, leek my cleet!"

Angry voices flew at them from every direction, but Victor Rubel was his focus, Rubel with his hard, offensive cock still hanging out of his pants, stabbing into Helmut's straining boner.

"Every dick from Walla Walla to the West End of London is going to want my condoms," Rubel spat, humping their manhoods together.

"That's what you think!"

They rolled across the floor, through a puddle of what Helmut hoped was spilled lubrication, hitting one of the serving himbos in the shin. The surfer dude dropped his tray. Champagne glasses shattered, and another high-pitched shriek pierced the air.

Rising up from a tangle of sweaty limbs, a shaved head demanded, "Stop it! Stop it, at once! You're ruining our fun!"

"This blond goose-stepper and his companion would like to ruin everybody's fun," Rubel said. "All so they can keep your cocks in cast-iron condoms! But I plan to change all of that. We will begin to market fiercely, proclaiming our product across the Internet, television, print media, and from our new fleet of dirigibles—those enormous cock-shaped giants of the sky— floating through the heavens, like helium-filled dicks! No one and nothing will stop us. *Viva la Revolución!*"

Rubel, now on top, cast his face toward the masses and shook his fist for effect. His hairy, vein-webbed dick—so very ugly, the cock of a lesser being, a primate—rose upward in concert with Rubel's hand. Helmut seized the opportunity and threw his punch. Rubel doubled over, wheezing as all the breath inside him was forced out.

As he fell forward, driving his erection into the front of Helmut's pants, Rubel ejaculated. The pressure of the other man's weight grinding against him, a frottage lover's dream, a true cockfight, shedding sperm instead of blood, forced Helmut over the edge. The room erupted in explosions of fireworks only he could see and hear.

His dick was still squirting in his tuxedo pants when the gorillas dragged both adversaries off the floor. One of the pinstriped guards gripped Helmut's arm. The other held a red-faced Rubel, who swayed on unsteady feet.

"Break it up!"

Helmut's unloading cock still ruled him, and as it continued to erupt, so did his fists. Against Vanessa's protests, Lady Darbi's sobs, and the cacophony of excited voices that rose and fell with the action—some interested only in getting off, most suddenly attracted to the grand theater taking place at the outer orbit of the beds—Helmut swung.

The gorilla staggered back, clutching at his jaw, his other hand flailing, searching for support, and briefly finding it...on the length of cord holding the flotilla of balloons aloft.

The gorilla yanked. The mesh dropped. And then, so did the balloons.

Hundreds—nay, thousands—of red, white, and pink balloons drifted down from the ceiling. In this glorious cascade, this show that far surpassed anything else taking place in the vast room, the gathering fell silent, breathless. There was only the rubbery groan of balloons brushing their slick epidermises against one another, a slow, drifting cloud of color descending to kiss the earth, and a sense of the greatness soon to come.

Then, one of those balloons, one tiny falling star in a slow-moving meteor shower of thousands, exploded.

Pop.

Another followed, and another after that. Soon there were so many coming apart, it stung the ear to listen, and dazzled the eye to watch. Gleeful voices joined in, but their ecstatic chortles paled in counterpoint.

The kiss of rubber skin teased Helmut's flushed cheeks and forehead, bounced off the slope of his nose. The cannonade quickly drove him mad. He fumbled his pants open, dropping them to his ankles, baring his muscled ass for all to see. Extending his arms, he allowed himself to drop backward into the sea of balloons. Fuck Rubel. Fuck the company, the mission.

And fuck Vanessa—which was exactly what he planned to do again, as whips of hot and cold tore at his naked flesh, and supreme excitement engulfed him.

BREATHING

Tenille Brown

It was a nice night for dying, a night when it was nice and warm out and the sky was dark and clear. That was what Renee wanted them to notice when they found her—that she had picked the most beautiful night of the summer to croak.

And her hair, well, it was absolutely darling. She had taken the time to curl it so that it framed her brown oval face and fell against her shoulders. She smelled nice, too, having splashed on perfume after she stepped out of the bath. Yes, Renee would look close to perfect on this lovely evening.

Renee knew that whoever found her would talk about it all. Like the fact that she had been watching the Home Shopping Network and the house still smelled like baked chicken. But the thing that would catch their attention, the one thing they would remember was that when they found her cold, stiff body, it would be clad in cheap blue latex.

The funny thing was, Renee didn't even like stretch material. It was misleading. It made the numbers inside the garments a lie.

An obvious size twelve could squeeze into an eight. A size four was suddenly a size negative-fucking-one.

But this dress had a corset top and Renee had a thing for corsets. And the dress was cute even if it was just a teeny bit slutty. She liked the way the black lace contrasted with the blue latex. She liked that the straps were wide on the shoulders, not those thin spaghetti things that couldn't even support an A cup.

And Renee had chosen blue because it was her favorite color and it looked good against her toffee skin. People told her that all the time. She could have gone with the black one, but black was too predictable—the color *was* synonymous with freak, after all—and red, well, red was just too trashy.

A tear trickled down Renee's cheek and she suddenly remembered she wasn't even wearing anything underneath. Not one of her lace bra and panty sets, not even the clean pair of cotton drawers her mother always told her to make sure she had on in case she had to go the emergency room.

It was never a question of whether Renee could pull the look off. She had long, strong legs, a slender waist thanks to a strict regimen of yoga and Pilates, and an ass that could rival a twenty-five-year-old's. Nothing needed lifting, pulling or tucking.

Hell. Renee Jones was a babe.

She was a babe who was smothering to death in her own bedroom.

And had the blessed zipper not gotten caught, had the slim waist of the garment not been halted by her boobs as she tried to pull it over her head, the dress might have looked damned good on her. Instead, it got stuck and covered her face so that she could hardly breathe through the tight material and now she found herself shuffling around her bedroom gasping for air.

These were things Renee thought about as her chest tightened and her breath caught in her throat. Beads of sweat gathered on her forehead and slipped down her temples.

And what put the cap on this utterly pathetic display of desperation was the fact that she and Keith had only been married six years and didn't need this yet. Their relationship didn't require extras like outfits and props. They were still fucking three, four times a week, and it was still pretty damned fresh, in her opinion.

Yes, the boys would think she was pretty in her interesting blue dress lying unconscious in her bedroom on this lovely night, Renee thought, as she drew a final breath and her eyes rolled and fluttered close.

The water was cold against Renee's skin. Her cheeks suddenly stung from the sharp contact of palm against skin. Her head rattled from the shaking.

"Are you okay, Renee? Can you catch your breath?"

The voice sounded distant but familiar to her.

She inhaled sharply. Then she coughed. Then Renee began to marvel at how much heaven looked like her very own bedroom and how closely this tall, broad-shouldered angel resembled her husband, Keith. It was a strange thing, death, a very strange thing.

"Renee! Re*nee*! What on earth were you doing? You know you could have killed yourself, don't you?"

Keith let go of her shoulders and Renee fell back onto the mattress, her head landing against the stack of pillows.

She licked her lips before she spoke. "Then you mean I *didn't* die?"

Keith sucked his teeth. Whatever concern he had had for her had been replaced with utter aggravation. "Of course you didn't die. You passed out is all."

He had taken off his jacket and loosened his tie. Keith rubbed the sweat from his face.

"Oh. Oh, good." It was all Renee could think to say, all she could think to do as she began tugging again at the cobalt blue latex that now rested snuggly around her torso, waist and hips.

Keith shrugged. "So, you want to explain yourself?"

Renee paused. "Explain what? The outfit or the situation?"

"Both." Keith's hands were on his hips. He began pacing the floor in front of her.

"Oh." Renee wrung her hands in her lap and crossed and uncrossed her legs at the ankles. "Okay, then, I'll tell you. But, Keith, before I tell you, you have to know that you're partially to blame for this, if not completely."

"Me?" Keith placed his finger to his chest, his soft brown eyes stretched wide. "I'm sorry. Did I get off work early to sneak over here and wrap blue latex around your head? Did I do it while you were sleeping, perhaps? Or did I knock you unconscious? Too much Court TV, Renee, way too much Court TV."

Renee folded her lips and tapped her feet against the hardwood floor. "Hear me out, okay?" she said. "And then you'll get what I'm saying."

Keith folded his arms. Renee wished he would sit down. He towered over her like a giant, and for once his stature didn't make her feel safe and protected. It made her feel foolish and small.

"Well," Keith said, his head cocked. And finally he sat down, easing his solid two hundred and twenty pounds onto the bed.

Renee exhaled. "Well, when we were out shopping the other day, and we were walking down Wagner Avenue—you remember?"

"Yes, Renee, now go on."

"Okay, and then that girl walked by." Renee halted then and waited for Keith's acknowledgment.

"What girl?"

Renee twisted her mouth and rolled her eyes. "You know what girl, Keith. That *girl*. The one that walked by with the skirt so short you could almost see her hooch."

"This is L.A., Renee," Keith said. "It would be a stranger thing to see a girl walk by who *wasn't* wearing a skirt chopped up to her—"

Renee threw her hand up at him and continued. "Anyway, the skirt was black and vinyl, and when she walked by you turned your head so fast I thought it was going to spin off your fucking shoulders."

Keith's mouth formed a thin, straight line. "Oh, her."

"Yes, her."

"So, then *she* made you do it?" Keith's serious face turned into a smirk.

"That's not what I'm saying, Keith. What I'm saying is when she strutted that twenty-two-year-old ass past us I thought we'd have to stop and get you a bib. You were damn near staggering, for Christ's sake!"

"Nonsense!"

"Really?"

"Yes!"

"Oh, *really*?"

"Okay, fine. I looked," Keith said. "Now, tell me what in the hell that has to do with this."

"Well, Keith, after that awesomely pathetic display of blatant boorishness, I figured I could find myself an outfit like that and maybe make you look at me that way. You used to, you know, and it didn't take a shred of garment to do it."

Renee waited for a response, and when there was none, she continued. "Anyway, I went into one of those shops during my lunch hour. You know, the ones always tucked into some back alley or right next to a strip club. And I saw this dress hanging up in the window and I thought you might like it."

Keith stepped back then and looked at the gathers of blue latex and black lace and string wrapped snuggly around his wife's body.

"Well, actually, I could like it," he said, "if I saw it on properly. You know, if it fit."

Renee's hands became frustrated fists at her sides. "Of course I didn't try the thing on, Keith. I was too embarrassed. I just saw one in a color that I liked and I just wanted to pay for it and get the hell out of there."

"Okay," Keith said, holding up his hands in defeat.

"And I wanted to surprise you by wearing it tonight...except I couldn't get the thing to zip all the way. Then, when I tried to force it up, it got stuck. So I just said to hell with it and decided to take the damned thing off. But when I started pulling it up, you know, trying to get it over my head since it clearly wasn't going over my ass, it got stuck and I couldn't breathe. I started panicking. I was seconds away from suffocating, Keith! Lord knows what might have happened if—"

"You were fine, Renee. You were fine the whole time." Keith fingered the thin blue material that lay against her body. "This stuff is completely breathable. They make it that way. You had a panic attack at most and fainted, that's it. Besides, if you felt like you were in that much danger, you could have called someone. Mrs. Frazier is always home, and Liv's right across the street, and the phone's right there beside you."

"Oh, sure," Renee said, her hand propped against her ear. "Hello, nine-one-one? Yes, I do have an emergency. You see, I seem to have gotten a little stuck in my new latex lingerie. Yes, yes, I know how absolutely absurd that sounds, but, you see, it was supposed to be *sexy*. Yes, sexy was what I was going for, *seductive,* and instead it's smothering the hell out of me. Yes, I'll need some help right away, thank you."

Keith stifled a giggle. "Okay, honey, I understand. Let's get you out of this thing, then."

"Thank you," Renee breathed.

She struggled to prop herself up on her elbows. Then her eyes fell to the display between her husband's legs.

"Keith?" Renee sat straight up then. "*Keith!*"

"*What?*"

"Do you have a hard-on?"

Keith cleared his throat and shifted his weight from one foot to the other. "Yes, Renee." he said. "Why, yes, I do."

"Oh, my *God!*" Renee's hands dropped to her lap, snapping loudly against the latex.

Keith sighed. "Well, what did you expect? I mean, that *was* what you were going for when you put the thing on, right?"

Renee shook her head. "Well, it was—then. But I had this whole other idea of how it was going to play out and I...then this...listen, I'm just not feeling that sexy anymore, all right?"

"All right, fine. Hold still while I pull." Keith knelt on the bed behind Renee and began tugging at the zipper on the back of the dress.

Keith pulled. Renee braced. He pulled and she arched. Keith pulled and the zipper went flying off.

"Oh, dear." His words were nearly a whisper.

Renee turned her head. "What? What happened?"

Keith reached for her shoulders and squeezed them gently. "Now, don't panic, but the zipper kind of broke. But don't worry. I'll just go get some pliers and I'll fix you right up."

Keith climbed off the bed and brought the pliers from the kitchen.

He pulled a bit, but when it didn't work, Renee exhaled and said, "Just cut it off."

Keith peeked around his wife's shoulders. "Cut it? Renee, are you sure?"

"Yes, just cut the fucking thing off, Keith. Let's just trash it and forget this whole thing ever happened."

Keith shrugged and went back into the kitchen, this time returning with the scissors. "Hold still," he said. "I don't want to jab you."

He placed the scissors against the tough material, but when he went to press the blades together, he suddenly halted.

Renee turned her head toward him. "What's wrong?"

Keith moved the scissors away and sighed. "I don't want to do it, Renee."

Renee grunted. "Well, why the hell not?"

"Because that would ruin it. And it's so pretty and all."

"Oh, pretty, Keith? Pretty? *Really*? Oh, yes, I'm sure that's what you like about it, the fact that it's pretty, the fact that it would make a fine outfit to wear to your next company luncheon. Look, sales are always final on lingerie. I couldn't even return it for store credit if I wanted. And hell, I've sweated and stunk up the fucking thing from here to eternity anyway. So, it's a lost cause."

Keith rested his chin on his wife's shoulder then. "I don't think it's such a lost cause and I think it smells pretty great, actually."

He lowered himself so that he lay on his belly across the bed and pressed his face into Renee's waist where the dress gathered and tucked. Renee felt him rub his nose across the lace.

"You've got to be kidding me," Renee said, more to herself than to Keith.

But he began to caress her ass, his moist fingers squeaking

across the latex. He reached down into the back of the dress where the zipper had caught and rubbed the small of her back. The latex snapped sharply against her ass when he pulled.

And though it could very well have been that her airway had been constricted for so long that she was now delirious, Renee felt certain that she liked it.

Then Keith began to speak, uttering words between touches and kisses. "You know, Renee," he said, "if you really want to be cut out of this thing right now, I can go on and do that, but I'm thinking maybe we should get your money's worth out of it since there's that pesky no-return policy on lingerie, anyway. Right?"

"Right," Renee said, her breathing suddenly heavy. "No return."

She grabbed Keith's wrist and guided his hand beneath her dress. She marveled at the smile that spread across his face when he discovered that she was bare underneath.

His fingers found their way inside her. With his free hand he tugged at the top of the dress so that her breasts were completely exposed. He took one into his mouth, licking and sucking while his fingers caused her back to arch and her thighs to tremble.

Keith paused only long enough to find his way out of his shirt and trousers. He maneuvered his boxers over his hips, pushed them down his thighs and kicked them off.

Then he grabbed the dress on both sides and jerked it up above her hips. The latex popped against her skin. He climbed up Renee's body and eased into her, rubbing his hands against her shoulders, her back, her thighs. He moved on top of her, the latex rubbing roughly against his skin.

Renee wrapped her legs around Keith's hips and lifted her own to draw his cock deeper inside her. She pulled and clenched, matching his moves with her own until finally the two of them were still, the hot, wet latex dress bonding their bodies together while they took deep breaths and slept.

In the middle of the night, Renee snuggled against Keith. She felt her crumpled dress tighten and pull against her midsection.

She pulled at it, trying once more to maneuver her way out of it. It snapped. It popped. Then finally, it ripped.

Renee stretched her now exposed brown body, the tips of her fingers grazing the headboard. She curled up, reached over and caressed the cool lump that rested between Keith's legs.

"I'm free, honey," she whispered into his ear. "The dress is off. You want to celebrate?"

Keith smiled and opened his eyes. He kissed Renee's lips. "Sure," he said. "Celebrate, sure." He pulled the torn latex dress from beneath her ass and held it tightly in his hand. He brought it up to his face.

He rubbed.

And sniffed, breathing the wondrous blue latex.

Then, he rose.

ABOUT THE AUTHORS

CRYSTAL BARELA's short stories can be found in the anthologies *Rode Hard, Put Away Wet: Lesbian Cowboy Erotica, Blood Sisters: Lesbian Vampire Erotica, Call of the Dark: Erotic Lesbian Tales of the Supernatural, Ultimate Lesbian Erotica 2006, Travelrotica for Lesbians* and *Locked & Loaded*. Look for her stories in the forthcoming *Lipstick on Her Collar, Screaming Orgasms and Sex on the Beach* and *Drag Kings*. Crystal is a staff writer for CustomEroticaSourcecom. Crystal enjoys spending time with her true love, as well as hiking and photography. You can email her at erotikryter@gmail.com.

TENILLE BROWN's writing appears online and in such anthologies as *A Is for Amour, Naughty or Nice, Sex and Candy, The Greenwood Encyclopedia of African American Women Writers, Iridescence,* and *Dirty Girls*. She obsessively shops for shoes, hats and purses and keeps an online blog on her website, www.tenillebrown.com.

ELIZABETH COLDWELL is the editor of the U.K. edition of *Forum*, and has had stories in a number of anthologies, including *Best SM Erotica 1* and *2*, *Sex and Shopping* and *Leather, Lace and Lust*. She has always been intrigued by the idea of a rubber football kit.

ANDREA DALE's stories have appeared in *Naughty or Nice*, *Cowboy Lover*, and *Screaming Orgasms and Sex on the Beach*, among others. With coauthors, she has sold novels to Cheek Books (*A Little Night Music*, Sarah Dale, 2007) and Black Lace Books (*Cat Scratch Fever*, Sophie Mouette, 2006). Her website is at www.cyvarwydd.com.

JEREMY EDWARDS is a pseudonymous sort of fellow whose efforts at spinning libido into literature have been widely published online. His work has also appeared in anthologies offered by Cleis Press, Xcite Books, and other print publishers. Jeremy's greatest goal in life is to be sexy and witty at the same moment—ideally in lighting that flatters his profile. Readers can visit him at http://www.myspace.com/jerotic or contact him at jerotic@gmail.com.

SHANNA GERMAIN's short stories and poems have been widely published in places like *Absinthe Literary Review*, *Best American Erotica*, *Best Bondage Erotica*, *Best Gay Romance*, *He's on Top* and *Slave to Love*. Read more of her work online at www.shannagermain.com

Writer **STELLA HUNTER-SMITH** shares a home in Louisiana with her lover and two German shepherds. This is her first literary swim in the pool of erotica.

JESSICA LENNOX has lived coast to coast and currently resides in New Jersey. Besides her love for writing, she is hopelessly addicted to video games and can often be found playing them on her computer and cell phone. Other hobbies, interests and obsessions include gender theory, motorcycles, travel, sports, and, of course, books! Her work has been published in *Best Women's Erotica 2008* and *Tales of Travelrotica for Lesbians: Erotic Travel Adventures 2.*

GREGORY L. NORRIS is a full-time professional writer who routinely contributes to a number of national magazines and fiction anthologies. Until recently, the idea for "The Balloonatics" was little more than a few rough lines on a notecard in his catalog of unwritten story ideas and had been bouncing around inside the gray metal recipe box since the summer of 1990, along with over two hundred of its as yet unborn siblings.

RADCLYFFE is the author of over twenty-five lesbian novels and anthologies, including the 2005 Lambda Literary Award–winners *Erotic Interludes 2: Stolen Moments,* edited with Stacia Seaman, and *Distant Shores, Silent Thunder.* She has selections in multiple anthologies, including *Best Lesbian Erotica 2006* and *2007, After Midnight, Caught Looking: Erotic Tales of Voyeurs and Exhibitionists, First-Timers, Ultimate Undies: Erotic Stories About Lingerie and Underwear,* and *Naughty Spanking Stories from A to Z 2.* She is the recipient of the 2003 and 2004 Alice B. Readers' award for her body of work and is also the president of Bold Strokes Books, a lesbian publishing company.

JEAN ROBERTA teaches first-year English classes at a prairie Canadian university and writes in several genres. Her erotic stories have appeared frequently on the illustrated website

Ruthie's Club and in over fifty print anthologies, including *Lust* (Cleis), *H Is for Hardcore* (Cleis), and *Best New Erotica 6* (Robinson, U.K.). Her reviews appear monthly on the website Erotica Revealed.

TERESA NOELLE ROBERTS has turned speculating obsessively about sex into a career. Her erotica has appeared in *Caught Looking: Erotic Tales of Voyeurs and Exhibitionists, Ultimate Lesbian Erotica 2007, B Is Bondage, E Is for Exotic, F Is for Fetish, H Is for Hardcore, He's on Top, She's on Top,* and other anthologies with equally provocative titles. She also writes with a coauthor under the name Sophie Mouette; look for Sophie's erotica in *Best Women's Erotica 2007,* Fishnetmag.com, *Caught Looking,* and various *Wicked Words* anthologies from Black Lace Books. Sophie's novel *Cat Scratch Fever* was published by Black Lace books.

THOMAS S. ROCHE's short stories have appeared in several hundred anthologies, magazines and websites, including four volumes of the *Best American Erotica* series. His ten published books include the short-story collections *Dark Matter, His,* and *Hers,* as well as three volumes of the *Noirotica* series and four anthologies of horror/fantasy fiction. He blogs and podcasts at www.thomasroche.com.

LILLIAN ANN SLUGOCKI, an award-winning feminist writer, has created a body of work on women and their sexuality that includes fiction, nonfiction, plays and monologues that have been produced on Broadway, Off-Broadway, Off-Off-Broadway and on National Public Radio. Her work has been published in books, journals, anthologies, and online, including Salon.com. She has been reviewed in the *New York Times,* the *Village Voice,*

Art in America, the *New Yorker,* the *Daily News,* the *New York Post,* and recently in London in *Time Out,* the *Guardian,* the *Daily Telegraph* and the *London Sunday Times.*

JAY STARRE, residing on English Bay in Vancouver, Canada, writes fiction for gay men's magazines, including *Men* and *Torso,* and has also contributed to more than forty anthologies, including *Travelrotica, Manhandled, Bear Lust* and *Bad Boys.*

Called "a trollop with a laptop" by *East Bay Express,* and a "literary siren" by Good Vibrations, **ALISON TYLER** is naughty and she knows it. Ms. Tyler is the author of more than twenty-five explicit novels, and the editor of thirty-six anthologies, including *A Is for Amour, B Is for Bondage, C Is for Coeds, D Is for Dress-Up, E Is for Exotic, F Is for Fetish, G Is for Games* and *H Is for Hardcore* (all from Cleis Press). In all things important, Ms. Tyler remains faithful to her partner of over a decade, but she still can't choose just one perfume. Visit her at www.alisontyler.com, or be her friend at http://myspace.com/alisontyler.

RAKELLE VALENCIA is the coeditor of the anthologies *Rode Hard, Put Away Wet, Hard Road, Easy Riding; Lipstick on Her Collar;* and *Drag Kings: Tales of Lesbian Erotica.* She has stories published in *E Is for Erotica, H Is for Hardcore, Cowboy Lover, Got a Minute?, Blood Sisters, Red Hot Erotica, Ultimate Lesbian Erotica 2005, 2006, 2007, The Good Parts: Pure Lesbian Erotica, Best Lesbian Love Stories 2005, Hot Lesbian Erotica 2005, Best Bondage Erotica 2, Best of Best Lesbian Erotica 2, Naughty Spanking Stories from A to Z, Best Lesbian Erotica 2004, 2005, On Our Backs: The Best Erotic Fiction Vol. 2,* and the magazine *On Our Backs.* Rakelle was also a 2006 semifinalist in the Project: Queer Lit contest.

KRISTINA WRIGHT is a full-time writer whose erotic fiction has appeared in over fifty anthologies, including four volumes of *The Mammoth Book of Best New Erotica*, two editions of *Best Women's Erotica, She's On Top: Erotic Stories of Female Dominance and Male Submission* and *Lust: Erotic Fantasies for Women*. Her work has also been featured in e-zines such as Clean Sheets, Scarlet Letters and Good Vibes Magazine. Kristina holds a B.A. in English and a M.A. in humanities. For more information, visit her website www.kristinawright.com.

ABOUT THE EDITOR

RACHEL KRAMER BUSSEL (www.rachelkramerbussel.com) is an author, editor, blogger, and reading series host. She has edited or coedited over twenty books of erotica, including *Yes, Sir, Yes, Ma'am, He's on Top, She's on Top, Caught Looking, Hide and Seek, Crossdressing, Naughty Spanking Stories from A to Z 1* and *2, Sex and Candy, Ultimate Undies, Glamour Girls,* and the nonfiction collection *Best Sex Writing 2008.* Her work has been published in over one hundred anthologies, including *Best American Erotica 2004* and *2006, Best Women's Erotica 2003, 2004, 2006* and *2007,* Zane's *Succulent: Chocolate Flava II* and *Purple Panties, Everything You Know About Sex Is Wrong, Single State of the Union* and *Desire: Women Write About Wanting.* Her first novel, *Everything But...,* will be published by Bantam in 2008. She serves as senior editor at *Penthouse Variations,* and wrote the popular "Lusty Lady" column for the *Village Voice.*

Rachel has written for *AVN, Bust, Curve,* Fresh Yarn,

Gothamist, Huffington Post, Mediabistro, *Newsday, New York Post, Penthouse, Playgirl, San Francisco Chronicle, Time Out New York* and *Zink,* among others. She has been quoted in the *New York Times, Seattle Weekly, USA Today* and other publications, and has appeared on the "Berman and Berman Show," NY1 and Showtime's "Family Business." She has hosted the In the Flesh Erotic Reading Series since October 2005, about which the *New York Times*'s UrbanEye said she "welcomes eroticism of all stripes, spots and textures." She blogs at lustylady.blogspot.com and cupcakestakethecake.blogspot.com. Find out more about rubber, latex and PVC fetishism at http://rubbersex.wordpress.com